GETTING
PUBLISHED

*the text of this book is printed
on 100% recycled paper*

GETTING PUBLISHED

An Author's Guide to Book Publishing

by

David St John Thomas
&
Hubert Bermont

HARPER COLOPHON BOOKS
Harper & Row, Publishers
New York, Hagerstown, San Francisco, London

A hardcover edition was originally published by Fleet Press Corporation in 1973. It is here reprinted by arrangement.

First HARPER COLOPHON edition published 1974.

STANDARD BOOK NUMBER: 06–090382–1

78 79 80   12 11 10 9 8 7 6 5 4

NOTE

Every care has been taken in the writing of this book and many people have been consulted; but accuracy cannot be guaranteed on taxation and legal matters which are always subject to change.

CONTENTS

GETTING
PUBLISHED

1

INTRODUCTION

Definitive Non-Fiction

The main aim of this work is to give practical advice to the growing number of people who write a book in their spare time on a subject connected with their profession, job or hobby. The kinds of people this book is directed to are teachers writing textbooks for use in classroom or school library, graduates turning their PhD theses into books, scientists bringing their colleagues up-to-date on technical developments, economists or sociologists with views on problems past or present, amateur historians ready to publish part of their researches, do-it-yourself experts with practical experience to pass on . . . the list is endless. Gardeners write on gardening, travelers produce guide books, cat breeders describe special points, railway historians lovingly portray branch lines as they were in their steam heyday, naturalists report on the behavior of wild animals, doctors discuss diseases and their cure.

This objective, outward-looking kind of book is the authors' main concern, because the current great expansion of literature is in this sphere. But some aspects of writing and publishing are, of course, shared by books of all kinds, and possibly even new novelists or writers of children's stories will find that parts of this work are relevant. Established professional authors, too, will find a number of points useful or provocative, though it is assumed the reader is new to authorship—to have something to communicate but not to be practiced in the art of writing or in dealing with publishers.

There are of course many previous books on writing and publishing, but nearly all of them are either elementary textbooks or are concerned with fiction and *literary* work. Here is a middle-of-the road approach that will be useful to many authors who will never figure on the best-seller lists but whose books will give pleasure to substantial minority audiences.

Most publishers have to patiently explain time and again simple facts about turning a manuscript into a book, because these facts are not adequately covered in any of the available reference works. This book, therefore, is principally aimed to help shape good ideas into good books.

Author, Publisher, Printer and Bookshop

Most of this book assumes an elementary understanding of the roles of author, publisher, printer and bookshop. Yet publishing firms not infrequently receive orders to quote for printing manuscripts as though they were printers who merely accept the job submitted, rendering the bill at the end. So before starting, these are the basic facts for any who are in doubt—and the rest please skip.

An author is of course the writer of a book, but in the publishing world today he does not necessarily have that book published exactly as he first writes or conceives it. He writes to a publisher to discuss publication, and for a variety of reasons the publisher may ask for the book to be changed. The author may agree to undertake the revision himself; eventually, when the nature of the book has been mutually decided, the publisher's staff may do further revision. The author can decline to have any such interference with his work, or he may object to interference beyond a given point, and thus risk rejection of the book by that particular publisher. He should not, however, be surprised that the publisher dares to suggest making changes. The novelist, the poet or the author of *pure* literature in any form would of course not normally expect his publisher to have much say in the actual detailed contents and presentation. Work of such kind is too intimate a reflection of the author's personality. But here we are concerned with *applied* literature; non-fiction works on specific subjects are only literary in that language should be used to the best advantage in presenting the facts. There need be no lack of artistic feeling, but the subject matter comes first and it is more important that the subject be covered clearly, thoroughly and in a rational order than that the work is written in any particular style or with any special literary effects. While, therefore, the author is the creator, he will frequently be expected to adapt his baby in accordance with the publisher's assessment of what is needed—and what will sell.

A publisher is an entrepreneur who normally publishes books that he has accepted or commissioned at his own cost and risk, usually paying the author a royalty on sales. He designs the books, chooses the paper and the binding materials, and determines the timetable of production and all other details, though frequently the author's view is taken into account on certain matters. The actual processes of printing and binding are sub-contracted to printers and binders, though to the detailed specifications of the publisher. A few publishers own printing works, but even then the publishing and printing sides of the business are under different management and the printing side acts as sub-contractor working to the requirements of the publisher. Publishers often buy their own raw materials such as paper and have them consigned to printers. Once the books have been printed and bound their consignment to the book trade is again organized by the publisher. Some publishers have their own warehouses and fulfillment centers; others sub-contract the storage and fulfillment operations, never handling the bulk stock.

Bookshops buy almost exclusively from publishers on recognized terms and to a well-established pattern of trade, which for certain classes of business also involves wholesalers. Occasionally bookshops undertake publishing on their own account, and some publishers own bookshops as well as printing works; but even where there is common ownership, the processes of printing, publishing and bookselling are always segregated and demand very different skills.

A Warning

Any author in the accepted sense of the word arranges the publication of his book with a publisher. Some people, however, fail to find a publisher willing to accept their work; and a few then attempt to print and publish on their own account. Quite apart from the fact that a book rejected by a cross-section of commercial publishers is unlikely to pay its way, this operation usually ends in disaster. The amateur finds it difficult to give the right instructions to the printer, and too often chooses the wrong kind of printer. He is likely to be even vaguer over the trade and publicity aspects, failing for instance to understand the role of the book jacket for publicity purposes, and not knowing how the book's advent should be announced through the trade press to the wide world. Even if he does eventually produce a conventional book at the right kind of price, he will not have a representative soliciting orders for him at bookshops throughout the land (the reluctance of most booksellers to order for stock unless a representative calls on them has to be experienced to be believed), he will probably not be taken seriously even by those shops he may have time to call upon himself, and he will lack knowledge of export procedures.

Sometimes an author can successfully publish a pamphlet or booklet intended just for limited sale—such as a guidebook which would anyway appeal only to shops in his own home town which he can visit regularly, or a small work of interest to members of his profession or society which he can market by mail, using the membership mailing list or advertising in the specialist magazine. With such small, paper-covered works the stakes and expectations are comfortably low, and failure to find the national public library demand is irrelevant.

But with rare and small-scale exceptions, the author-publisher of a bound book will be dismissed as a crank; he will waste his money and other people's time. Any publisher hears pathetic tales of authors printing books and then trying to find a publisher to *publish* them; of elderly men putting their last savings into producing their life history and having to give up their front room to storing the unwanted stock; of authors who have paid publishers to produce works on their behalf with practically no sales resulting. There are of course circumstances in which it is recognized as sensible and reputable for authors to help finance their own specialist works; but there are also a few publishers with whom it is best not to make such arrangements. This aspect is dealt with in chapter 8.

Do You Have a Book in You?

But it would be wrong to end the introduction on a negative note. Ever more people from every conceivable walk of life are becoming successful authors, not because they have any special literary genius but because there is something they want to communicate or explain, and they have the determination and commonsense to bring a book to fruition. Many are rightly proud of their books. Some have won promotion in their jobs or professions as the result of publication, and others have acquired a high standing among followers of their hobby. Bank balances are also usually the happier for authorship, especially if the most has been made of opportunities to save tax.

Do you have a book in you? What tests should you apply? One might suggest this simple questionnaire:

(1)   Does your subject justify a book, or another book if others already exist? (Subject matter is discussed in chapter 1.)

(2)   Would you have the determination to complete research on

all aspects of the subject (including those that might least interest you personally) and to stick at the task of committing the material to paper?

(3) Have you a basic ability to write? (If you cannot write a letter without a struggle, you will obviously find authorship trying.)

(4) Are you sure your aims are sensible (that you are not, for instance, convinced that the world is waiting for your new economic theory that will result in immediate peace and prosperity everywhere)?

(5) Are you willing to be guided, and perhaps to adapt your approach, if a publisher thought that a change would open up a wider market?

If you answer these questions in the affirmative, there is little to stop you, and the task will probably prove less severe than you imagine. Enjoy yourself, and do not be discouraged by relations or friends who hint that your qualifications are inadequate.

2

SUBJECT MATTER
AND
APPROACH

2

SUBJECT MATTER AND APPROACH

With Publication in Mind

The surest way of writing a book that will not be published is to choose the wrong subject. That no commercial publisher will accept a text on the history of your central heating system, or a manual on methods of cutting bread and butter, is obvious. Yet it is almost as certainly a waste of time to pick a potentially promising subject and handle it irrationally. Not just the basic subject, but the whole balance of subject matter and the approach to it, require careful thought and planning.

The belief that *authors should write what they want* is irrelevant where non-fiction is concerned. Those who want to communicate with an audience necessarily hope to see their work *published*. Therefore they cannot entirely ignore the public's taste. They cannot ignore it even if they hope to influence it. However small the audience a writer has in mind, he must try to meet its needs, envisaging the use that potential readers could have for the book, and avoiding putting them off by including an unsuitable range of contents or by unnecessarily flouting publishing conventions. This holds true even if he is not in the least concerned with financial reward; he still has something to communicate and should be serving the interests of his readers.

Be honest about your objective in writing. Those who do it purely for their own amusement can set down what they choose without disciplined shape or scope. This can be an enjoyable occupation, like taking family snapshots or doing the occasional amateur painting. But do not pretend you are merely amusing yourself when in fact you have a wider audience in mind; or, if you are merely amusing yourself, do not blame the publishers who ultimately reject your work. Of course some creative writing may be eminently suitable for publication even though originally done purely for pleasure or in self-expression: some of the best children's stories began with a one-child audience; some novelists who became international figures cared little whether their work was published or not. But such spontaneous achievement is rare; most successful authors plan and execute their work with businesslike practicality, making every effort to put themselves in the reader's place. The chances are that if you want to see your words in print you will have to accept conventions—and accept that the plotting of words on paper is not automatically a form of pure art immune from commercial considerations.

This book is anyway primarily concerned with factual works, which account for an ever-growing proportion of the ever-increasing number of titles published each year. No anti-fiction bias should of course be inferred. Fiction will remain an indispensable means of communication and enrichment; even while writing this chapter a modern novel has been the background reading. But in the past there has been an artificial identification of *writing* with writing fiction; if your friends heard you were writing a book they assumed it was a novel. In his book *The Truth About Publishing*, published as long ago as 1926, Sir Stanley Unwin, director of one of England's leading publishing houses, complained about the automatic assumption that all books were fiction, and this tendency remains remarkably strong even today.

The Subject

The best subjects are those that come naturally—subject first and then the desire to write a book. Your professional work or your job may have brought you specialized knowledge of some aspect of your own field; you may be interested in the local canal, have delved into its history, amassed facts about it and the traffic it carried, and ended with a longing to communicate your enthusiasm to others, to provide them with the book you would have loved to read had it existed earlier. Maybe your hobby is a specialist branch of gardening or astronomy, gastronomy or photography, and you have practical advice that could be useful to others. You may have studied the works of specialists on an aspect of history or scientific research, philosophy or theology, and wish to make a synthesis of their findings in a broader-based book for a wider audience; you may have had the opportunity for some original research in laboratory or field, or to study documentary or other evidence which sheds new light on matters of interest to others. Or you may have travelled to a distant part of the world and have some topical or personal impressions worth sharing.

Many of us have at least one book in us, but anyone with a vague wish to write without any information to impart to any particular audience would be better employed in reading—and living—until a subject and an audience can be defined. So many who have the germ of a book in them fail to work out who the readers are likely to be (or whether they exist) and to orientate the work to please and interest them. The commonest mistakes in approach might be summarized thus:

(1) Being interested in writing only about what is already known personally or can be discovered easily, and thus failing to produce a viable subject coverage.

(2) Though coming closer to producing a viable subject coverage, marring it by giving unbalanced vent to some theory, love or hatred.

(3) Being unable to select a good balance of material and, for

21

instance, floundering when trying to put a local or limited subject in broader perspective, or giving too much minute detail and not enough general picture.

(4) Skimping the job, to speed publication and financial return, especially by failing to complete research on certain aspects.

Given the right command of subject knowledge, the writing of a book is not necessarily a difficult task. But it must be remembered that books are expensive to produce, and the purchaser paying perhaps eight dollars expects something more for his money than is provided by the daily paper or weekly magazine that costs fifty cents. Whereas in his newspaper or magazine he is probably satisfied with a fairly superficial and ephemeral coverage, plus perhaps odd items that he might clip out for later use, he will normally expect a book to have lasting value. He also expects it to hang together as a whole with adequate purpose and planning. For this very reason few collections of newspaper articles make satisfactory books— unless they are completely rewritten and reshaped, filling in any gaps.

Before you start writing, therefore, make sure that what you have to say warrants the expensive operation of book production. The obvious question is too frequently overlooked: would you yourself, or would your relations or friends with similar interests, be prepared to pay the conventional price of a hardback book to read what you have to say? Note the word hardback, since few works are issued as inexpensive paperbacks until they have first made good in hardback form.

Perhaps the manuscripts that publishers are most tired of receiving are personal memoirs. So many people want to start writing about themselves: yourself is, after all, the subject closest to you. It is an easy subject since it requires little if any research; you may come close to complete accuracy, and if you do not, probably no one will know. There is only one snag: generally other people will not find your life and thoughts, once presented in cold print, as all-absorbing as you may do. Publishers receive an enormous number of unsolicited manuscripts of a strictly

22

personal nature. They come not from famous people, but from ordinary men and women—the story of my personal travels in Europe, my life in the army and what I have done since, how I came to take over my rival's business, how I live with my husband, how we converted a farmhouse together, how I solved the mystery of the universe, what we think about this, that and the other. People even offer manuscripts interpreting their own dreams.

By no means is all this flood of paper totally uninteresting, but very few of the manuscripts have sufficient value as a whole to warrant publication in hardback form at the inevitable high price. The best manuscripts in this personal category are of course by those whose lives and experiences really have been outstanding and are therefore genuinely worth communicating in detail, or by those who (while using their personal experiences as the book's backbone) concentrate on objective details, for instance, giving plenty of hard practical advice for others while telling of their difficulties in converting a henhouse into a holiday cottage. Conversely, the utterly unpublishable manuscripts are by those who lack all modesty—or is it judgment? Does the engine driver who might perhaps find an interested audience for accounts of his work on the pedal really expect readers also to want to hear about his work as usher at the local church, how he cooked his Christmas turkey and his views on modern youth?

Personal and family jokes and experiences seldom stand up to presentation to the wide world. Have you never been bored by a friend's display of his holiday photographs—and he, after all, is someone you know? Of course generalizations are dangerous, and a few reminiscences will always appear in the bestseller lists, but if you want to see your first book published you will probably be wise to make it as impersonal as possible, treating an objective subject in an objective way.

An industrialist wrote a good manuscript on the rise of his own industry but included quantities of irrelevant personal matter. Such was his role in the growth of the industry that he was probably the only person qualified to tell the complete story, and the use of the personal pronoun and of personal touches had to be fairly extensive. But never was a man more incredulous than he was at being told that though people would be interested in his working life because of the light it shed on the story of the industry concerned, they would not want all the odds and ends of information about his religious beliefs or his children's escapades. His publisher tried to persuade him to scrap this and instead fill in the earlier history of his industry which he did not know at first hand and had therefore omitted. "I cannot believe that people will be more interested in how —— was first manufactured than in my life details," he said.

So try to place yourself in strangers' shoes and be as objective as possible. If you do have some personal material that will, even in cold print, interest the wide world, wrap it up and put it in its proper context. Thus, while part of the narrative may come easily from memory, you will probably be involved in research to complete the picture. And that, indeed, is the case with most books. It is generally only the superficial sketch that can be written from start to finish without some checking or research.

While other people can write about themselves, and publishers are daily inundated with autobiographies, personal travel tales and the like, you may have it in your power to write the only book on a particular aspect of a factual subject. Such a book may appear to be very specialist and limited in appeal, but if it is the only one it will command a fairly high price (perhaps twice as much per page as an autobiography) and it should have a long life, perhaps being reprinted every few years for a couple of decades. It is often these quiet, solid books of reference value, those that perhaps take the longest to research and write, that live longest and pay the most handsome dividends in the end.

The Approach and Coverage

As well as undertaking research on the less familiar aspects of his subject, an author does need to bring enthusiasm to the task of making his coverage as complete as possible. Forgetting all about finance, the work should be *editorially viable.* It should set out to cover fully a rational subject span, even though this will involve the author in dealing with some matters that he does not find as interesting as others. With the general rise in education standards, and indeed with the increase in the number of non-fiction titles being published, a book must have an adequate *raison d'etre.* Tastes are becoming ever more sophisticated, and there is little room now for the often ill-assembled hodge-podge that were accepted in the earlier years of the century.

Let us take the example of a person absorbed by the history of a local tribe of Indians in his state. Until about 1940, such books that were published consisted largely of a general history and possibly an account of any encounters or dealings that the author had with the members of the tribe. Basically it would be a book based on some personal interviews and observations by the author strung together in a continuous narrative. Such works were not without charm, and some include information which remains useful to this day. But they were poorly planned, and little if any attempt was made at a definitive, all-round account of any particular aspect of the tribe's history and evolution (religious ritual, commerce, etc.) let alone its entire history. Neither the author nor the publisher exercised much discipline; generally publishers rejected such books outright or accepted them just as they stood.

Today's writer will have to be far more systematic in his approach. He will probably gather the material for the basic skeleton in a matter of weeks or months, but considerable application over a long period will be needed to clothe it with the details of the sociology, mythology, anthropology, demography, ecology, economy and religion of the Indians in question. He will have to search for and study books and records in libraries and record offices as well as any other evidence that he can find anywhere. His task will not be complete until he has tapped and synthesized all possible sources of information.

Moreover, even when he has covered all aspects of the chosen tribe itself, he will have to make sure he knows enough about neighboring tribes that may have affected its history and culture; and he will still have to make sure that he can tell the story with adequate regional and national perspective. He must discover in just what ways this tribe differed from others, so that he does not tire readers who may know more about Indians than he does. And if he is not prepared to do all this, it is better that he does not attempt the task at all—or at any rate does not expect publication in hardback form. It is no use for him to offer a pot-pourri of just what happens to interest him personally, though within reason certain aspects or periods will probably be given more thorough coverage than others.

Many subjects are more difficult to define than the history of Indians and different people may well justify covering different segments of material. But the point about editorial viability still holds. A book should set out to cover some rationally-defined subject or segment of it, and do it thoroughly. To take an extreme example, there may be a case for dealing only with the earlier history of a city, or perhaps only with the later history, but you cannot rationally justify covering 1875 to 1920 and 1930 to 1970 on the grounds that the ten-year intervening administration "did not do anything." If you write a book about a state, you may possibly produce some justification for barely mentioning an extreme area adjoining the next state but you cannot ignore a large town in the middle because you do not happen to like it or know anything about it.

You can of course exercise a balanced personal preference. You can pause in close-up on an aspect that happens to appeal strongly. You can admit that you are giving only a broad outline of another aspect which has perhaps been covered better by another book. You may be able to change the whole purpose of the book originally envisaged so as to make it editorially viable: for instance, if you find that you want to devote three-quarters of a book on the South to its literary history and associations, then why not plainly make it and label it a book on Southern literary history. If you are only interested in a certain aspect of a bigger subject, it is often best to define that area and keep to it; this at least will mean that you do not offer a publisher an apparently

26

wider-ranging book which he rejects because its subject coverage is unbalanced.

Even if the whole aim of your book is to put forward some particular viewpoint or theory, a sensible subject range is still essential. While you will naturally make the best of such material as supports your contention, you will only weaken your case if you deny the existence of counter-evidence. In all works where the author's personal view is being projected, it pays to make abundantly plain what is being offered as objective fact and what is personal interpretation. It is too easy to overstate the case even if you do not tamper with the actual evidence, and the reader's confidence may be harder to regain than it was to lose.

As tastes become more sophisticated, in all ways greater care must be taken to prevent inadvertently insulting the reader's intelligence. Fortunately these days few authors resort to slices of imaginary dialogue to cover up a lack of fact, but some are not above indulging in guesswork where the factual evidence is not readily available, and others still introduce irrelevant padding. Topographical works have been among the worst offenders here; until the 1950s many were just scissors-and-paste compilations stuck together with the author's comments on anything under the sun. Two points might usefully be made about them. Firstly, many were designed only for light reading and entertainment, and in days of cheap book production there was an adequate market to make such ephemera commercially worthwhile. Today, however, people obtain their entertainment more cheaply in other ways—such as looking at television, reading the free color supplements that come with the weekend newspapers and buying paperbacks. (The price difference between a new topographical book making its first appearance in hardback and a paper-covered reprint of popular fiction and other proved successes is far greater now than a generation ago.) Then, secondly, so much topography was of so poor a quality that many younger people dismissed the subject as a whole as being of little interest to them until a new generation of more purposeful works began appearing.

Many new authors are puzzled about how to present their

material when a previous book covering basically the same subject is already on the market. The proper answer is surely that a good work should always be complete, self-contained. It may refer the reader to more specialist tomes to discover more detail on certain facets, but a new book is invalidated if the reader is expected to consult a previous work in order to be able to understand and appreciate it. Like most points in this chapter, this may seem obvious: if you are claiming that your new book is more useful than the heavy-going works that have preceded it, do not get out of covering a difficult aspect of the subject by saying that one of these predecessors does it better. Only the reader who wants to range deeper or wider than the context of your book allows should be referred to other works.

Check Before You Start

Certainly before you start writing you should check what other books exist on the same subject. Most publishers have had experience of authors writing in ignorance of the literature already available. There may well be room for another volume, but at least you should know what has gone before and consider how your contribution can be different and better.

If you know a librarian or anyone at an institution which might use your book, or members of the profession or followers of the hobby for whom the work is intended, it may be useful to discuss your basic plan at an early stage, and to note special requirements for reference material, illustrations, length and price. Certain types of books have conventionally to be published at fairly low prices, which limits their length and therefore their scope, and this may make you realize you are undertaking the impossible—or perhaps have two books instead of one. Incidentally, the librarian's or another expert's views on any previous books on the same subjects can be useful. Maybe previous authors omitted or over-emphasized certain aspects; or maybe you will learn that a previous book stands in such high esteem that there is little point in proceeding along the lines you had first fixed.

But do not be downcast when you hear that someone else has almost finished writing the book you are planning. Very many more books are planned than written; many more are started than finished; many more are finished than published; and many more are published than really succeed in their aim. You might be unlucky, but statistically it is likely that the threatened opposition will not materialize, or that the book will in fact be quite different from yours. Probably your rival has been on the point of finishing (or starting?) for the past five years.

There is one further thing you should do before you start the actual writing: plan the book in detail and make sure that you can tackle all the material that has to be included to give proper subject coverage. That does not necessarily mean collecting all the material before you make a beginning; but you need to know that it does exist and is accessible to you, and that you are capable of absorbing and synthesizing it. A short synopsis is essential. It may consist of only a dozen or so headings scribbled on a cigarette packet or scrap of newsprint, but it will prove surprisingly useful. Quite apart from the fact that an assessment of the overall plan will make for easier and more orderly writing once you start, it will pinpoint weaknesses in your approach and material. It may make you realize that unless you devote your next holiday to research on a particular point in a certain record office, the execution of the whole book will be delayed. It may even make you realize that you are attempting the impossible, resulting in your cutting down the scope or turning to a different subject.

Some subjects are inevitably difficult to handle; before you commit yourself to the project, perhaps invite the interest of a publisher and tell your colleagues and friends of your plan; make sure you can bring it off. A high credibility rating is one of the author's strongest assets; do not lose it at the beginning of your literary career by announcing things you cannot accomplish. You will sink even in your own estimation and that of your wife (or husband) who in all probability will have much to

29

bear while you are *in labor.*

The Title

Most people also like to decide on a title before starting. A good, clear, telling title is more important than it used to be. This again is partly because tastes have become more sophisticated, and today an oblique or obscure title for a non-fiction book usually seems as naive as a piece of imagined coversation devised to *make the book more interesting.* It is also partly because with the increasing avalanche of new books it becomes ever harder for booksellers and librarians to digest and remember new titles, and the more contrived the title the less likely it is to register.

Some books defy a nice neat title. If you cannot adequately convey the scope of the work in the title proper, try a combination of a short, snappy title and a longer, descriptive subtitle. If you cannot succeed in labeling the work even then, should you be writing it at all? Should its structure and aim be simplified? If you cannot describe it briefly, how will others do so? Remember that advertising space is expensive, and your publisher will not be able to afford an essay to describe your book's basic aims in the press, even if the public would read it. There are many well-known exceptions, but generally the book that is difficult to describe is also difficult to sell.

The title may be changed and improved along the route . . . but at least establish the possibility of finding a suitable label before you commit yourself to writing a book.

What Is Your Market?

Just as you define your subject, you must define your market. The main one is probably fairly obvious, but without jeopardizing your book's success there, can you do anything to widen the appeal? The result could be to double your sales and your number of readers.

For example, can an academic book on say a scientific subject be written and presented so that it will also appeal to more amateur scientists without damaging the work's academic standards? The avoidance of technical jargon, and the weaving in of odd explanations to help the uninitiated in a way that will not offend experts who already know, will go a long way to help. If you have a wider audience in mind, take care to avoid a display of the fact that you know far more than the reader. Do not assume he knows previous works on the same subject, and if referring to these do so by title as well as by author—eg "As Smith says in his *Basic Elements*" is kinder to the nonspecialist reader than just "According to Smith." If there is a possibility of a fairly wide general sale, it can also be sensible to consolidate the footnotes at the end of the book, with adequate cross-referencing between them and the text; some non-academic readers—and bookshop managers—are discouraged by the presence of a large number of notes mixed in with the text. But if your interest in writing the book is solely to raise your status in the academic world, you may want to follow the traditional academic practices in these matters and not worry about possible lost sales—providing your publisher does not mind the lost sales either.

The requirements of general and specialist readers can often be partially reconciled by concentrating certain specialist and very technical information into tables, appendices or self-contained paragraphs which can be skipped by those not interested. Adequate headings and general signposting can also do a lot to render a specialist book intelligible to the layman.

Then, are you writing for adults or for children? Especially in fields like popular science and natural history, the division is far less sharp than it used to be, and it is often possible to combine both markets by using simple, direct language, sticking to the point and explaining technical terms—in an unpatronizing kind of way. No playing-down is required for the juvenile reader (his powers of comprehension in scientific and natural history matters are anyway often greater than assumed).

Diagrams and pictures can obviously help, as again can the consolidation of optional-extra technical material into self-contained paragraphs, tables and appendices. Many educational textbooks are today presented as straightforwardly as standard adult non-fiction titles and can therefore be published in trade editions for sale through bookshops as well as in special textbook editions for school and college use.

Then, are you writing for a local, national or international audience? Widening the scope here can dramatically increase sales. Taking the example of a history of a single town, if you concentrate entirely on local matters, dutifully chronicling the doings of local bigwigs, with lists of mayors and councilmen, the history can only serve people with some concentrated interest in that town. If, however, you project your town as an example of similar places throughout the country, or a part of the country, and show how it fits into regional or national trends, how it was affected by outside influences and what influence it had on general trade and commerce, there will be at least a small market elsewhere.

In the case of books of regional interest, the larger the region the greater the potential sale, not merely because the book will then cover an area of greater population and more bookshops, but because the wider scope may open up a stronger national and even international market. Thus a book on tobacco-growing in the United States would have a British sale in a way that a book on tobacco-growing in one section of North Carolina would not. Or need your regional book be a regional one at all? For instance, a manuscript on *Growing Rarer Shrubs and Trees in New England* is readily convertible into *Growing Rarer Shrubs and Trees*. A book with "New England" in its title might never gain national circulation.

Widening the interest still further, can the book appeal to a substantial overseas as well as home market? This is where the greatest reward may be obtained. Many books have a potential British and other overseas sale, but this is frequently lost. Sometimes it is lost because the author failed to include some British material that would have helped promote the book

32

across the Atlantic, or because he failed to check his British or Australian facts as carefully as his American ones. Occasionally British prospects are thrown away by an author going out of his way to be anti-British or generally xenophobic. More often authors simply fail to appreciate the possibilities of overseas sales, drawing all their examples from the United States and introducing place names, slang terms and money sums that can only be understood by an American reader. Adaptation of a few dozen sentences might render a book acceptable overseas, but once the work has been published the opportunity for a special British edition may have been reduced. Remember in what parts of the world English is spoken and read, and do not put necessary obstacles in the way of international circulation. Translation is a different matter, since a translated book has to be reset, adjustments can be made at that stage; but a British publisher, after seeing the manuscript, might well be willing to share the typography costs with the American publisher for the right to produce his own edition in England.

The Quantity of Fact

A non-fiction book does not have to be wholly solemn, let alone characterless; even though you may use the personal pronoun sparingly, quite a bit of your character may emerge incidentally. The work may be fun to write and fun to read. But never be ashamed of keeping to the facts. The dramatized-documentary approach is usually less telling than the straight-forward documentary. Unless you are a Thornton Wilder (in which case you are unlikely to be discouraged by anything said here), you will make the history of your real town sound a great deal more interesting and convincing than that of an imaginary one. But what you do, do thoroughly; even in narrow selfish terms, twice the labor may bring you three times the income and respect. One accepted standard work is worth many pot-boilers.

One other point is worth making. Writing a specialist book

can be a lonely business, since few of your relatives or friends may be able to comprehend it or its aims. The temptation to please friends and relatives by taking their advice to make the work less technical and more easily digestible is real; but remember that they are probably not the kind of people who would ever go out and buy or borrow that type of book. They are not your market. Forget them and stick to writing for the people who share your kind of interest and will positively pay for reading your work. If the book sells steadily through successive editions, your esteem will rise among your acquaintances even if they have not the foggiest idea what it is all about, what could have made you write it, or why other people read it.

3

THE MECHANICS
OF
WRITING

THE MECHANICS OF WRITING

Planning

For people who come to authorship because they have something specific they want to communicate, and not because they want to exercise the art of communication for its own sake, the actual writing of the book can be a wearisome business. Each author has to discover largely through trial and error what methods suit him best. Indeed, writing is such an individual matter that at first it might seem merely fatuous to chatter brightly on how best to set about it. There are, however, certain broad avenues of approach which help reduce frustration and wasted labor.

It undoubtedly helps to begin by appreciating that the process of committing original material to paper is demanding. It tends, moreover, to make demands on your family as well as yourself: not only may you be tired and irritable after a writing session, but you may have to curtail the family's noise-making, have time for fewer outings, and make everyone in the house acutely aware that you are at work.

Most experienced writers like to keep the agony to the

minimum by making a clear-cut distinction between the time spent on research and planning before writing, or on revision afterwards, and the actual creative period in the middle. Too many part-time authors go to their desk on a Friday evening or a Sunday morning without a crisp objective, and waste time in a muddle of mixed tasks. If they kept to a definite plan, they could make life less strained for themselves and those around them, could probably get the job done more quickly—incidentally increasing their earnings—and keep the promised delivery date to the publisher!

While engaged on the central creative task of committing your material to paper, you will be fully stretched. The job genuinely requires an unusually tense discipline and concentration—and especially if you are not used to the art of communication, nothing is more discouraging than the sight of blank pieces of paper that somehow you have to fill. When you are *in labor*, you may justifiably regard yourself as a maestro commanding three times your ordinary hourly rate of pay. But once this superman has been engaged, do not toy with minor details of research that can be added later in a more relaxed mood. If during these periods of highly-concentrated work you are helped by being spoiled with music, unlimited quantities of luxurious copy paper, coffee or whatever, then indulge yourself—provided again that all this applies just to the period of creative writing and not to the longer and more mundane periods of research and revision.

It follows that well before you get down to the actual writing sessions, you should not merely have completed your research and have all the material (especially quotations you want to use) available in handy form, but have worked out the book's general plan. Ideally there should be a detailed synopsis allotting all the material to specific chapters, and even quoting the order of ingredients within the individual chapters; but whether you have a formal synopsis, make do with headings written on a cigarette packet, or merely keep the general scheme at the back of your head, you should know exactly what goes where.

Some people claim that they cannot produce a synopsis and would prefer just to start writing and "see how things turn out." Frankly, if you cannot work out a simple preliminary plan of attack, you are unlikely to be a good author. No film company can send off a director on location with the expensive film unit before he has planned what to shoot. Rather than spend valuable creative time on committing material to paper before you have a clear sense of direction, it is probably better to go to the other extreme and set yourself a definite target of how much to write, or what particular aspects to cover, in a given time. At least you are less likely to succumb to distractions, and if your wife knows that you are really hard at work and will have something to show for it, she will find it easier to keep the family temporarily quiet and your friends at bay.

Once under way do anything to avoid interrupting the flow of words. Refuse to become bogged down in the first paragraph; the important thing is to let the narrative start telling itself. The introduction can be considered later. Often enough the first paragraph over which you may have struggled for half a day seems redundant when you finish the chapter: many book chapters, like newspaper articles, are stronger shorn of their concluding sentence or so as well as their introductions, though these may have taken longest to compose.

Leave gaps for any statistical or reference details you suddenly remember are not yet at hand, and do not worry about the odd ugly sentence slipping through. *Keep the narrative on the move*, even at the expense of leaving a line or two of gibberish where you have to explain a ticklish point; once the rest of the chapter is completed it will be much easier to smooth out or entirely rewrite any troublesome passages.

Order and Continuity

Writing sessions need to be as long as possible since the beginning of each session is used on becoming reacclimatized; often three-quarters of the output comes in the last half of the time. Also, pack in as many sessions as you can until a natural break in the book is reached, for continuity is vitally important. From this point of view the easiest books are those with self-contained chapters; providing you can keep continuity within each chapter, gaps between them do not matter. But where a strong continuous thread runs—or should run—through a complete book, as in a closely argued scientific or historical work, the ideal is to live with the work until the whole rough draft is completed. Incidentally, professional journalists are among those who find it hardest to attain continuity; not only are they used to writing self-contained pieces seldom exceeding 1,500 words, but the routine journalistic output which must go on alongside book-writing, with probably erratic working hours, gives a divided loyalty. With honorable exceptions, their books tend to lack sustained writing and to be made up of staccato self-contained sections.

A carefully thought-out synopsis should of course help produce continuity of theme as well as enable you to make the best use of your writing time. Even if you find it easier to write the chapters in a different order from what is finally intended, the synopsis will help control the selection of material to be included or excluded each time. For a variety of reasons it may be easier to start in the middle of the book, and indeed there is much to be said for tackling the easiest chapters first. The difficult portions, perhaps especially the introduction, then tend to look less forbidding when you reach them.

The question of order of contents is so important that a muddle here is the one hitch that should be allowed to halt a creative writing session. It has been suggested that leaving gaps for missing material, or passing bungled explanations in the rough draft, to enable the writing to be kept on the move. But if the basic order is sliding awry, the trouble of sorting it out later may be worse than that of stopping now. Of course this is a question of degree. If you recall that some fact or argument should have been added at a point you have already passed, it may be best to indicate the fact in the margin and go on. But if you have lost the sense of direction, then stop.

Be logical in the way you present your material. If your order of ingredients is illogical, you will find it hard to carry the reader with you: in his struggle to keep abreast with your main story or argument, he may miss the subtler points; or even worse he may be sidetracked by oddments and lose the main thread. Take care to make plain that a digression is a digression, and if for instance you are dealing with the United States Senate, do not suddenly switch to a potted biography of Huey Long as though he were the book's main subject.

Avoid fragmentation. Do not write down material just as it comes into your head, perhaps resulting in details about the same subject being irrationally peppered throughout long sections of the book. A good synopsis should ensure that the right aspects are thoroughly covered in the right chapters. But make sure that even within individual chapters or paragraphs, the order is logical. For instance, you may slip into an A, B, C, A, B, C pattern, twice working through basically the same sequence, possibly with a slightly different background or argument, but with the same facts relating to A, B and C still appearing in both sequences. Almost invariably logic is better served and space saved if all the matter about A is concentrated in one place before moving on to B.

Sometimes you may want to elaborate on material A to introduce both material B and material C, so that the order becomes A, B, A, C. Even if there is a logical link between A and C, unless you are a skilled and practiced writer it will be clearer to concentrate everything to do with A in one place. When you come to introduce material C, you can then either refer back to A or repeat an essential point making clear that it is a repetition. But no additional fact about A should be held back to provide the introduction to C.

If the A-C link seems as vital as the A-B one, you will probably have to accept that you cannot always convey to the reader every nuance of an argument without confusing him. You may be able to establish the additional link elsewhere; but even assuming that your readers have the same degree of comprehension as yourself, the progressions of material need to be as simple as possible, even at the expense of having to drop a supplementary point you would have enjoyed. (You can perhaps add a footnote as an optional extra for those willing to consider finer detail—a note that can be overlooked, at least at first, by readers concentrating on the basic theme.)

A fairly ruthless determination to streamline the progression of fact is particularly necessary when considering the chronological versus the subject approach in books with an historical content. Some of the most disappointing historical manuscripts have been by authors who could not decide which of these two approaches to adopt and who chopped and changed in mid-stream resulting in inexcusable fragmentation of material.

The subject approach is best, since the strictly chronological one in itself tends to disperse related facts. Take the case of a railroad history in which the author has to tell the story of a main line and that of several branch lines having junctions with it. If the chronological approach is adopted, there may be a dozen or more references to the development of any one branch line. Not merely may these references interfere with the flow of the narrative about the main line—and detract from its interest—but the story of the branch line may not come out clearly in its own right. If tne subject approach is adopted, the reader's attention will at one point be fully focused on the branch line and there will be a much better chance of describing its history, character, traffic and so on. It may of course be impossible to tell the story of the main line without some reference to the existence of the branch; in that case a suitable supplementary reference (probably quoting the page on which the main description will be found) can be included, but all the main facts about the branch will still be in one place.

Authors can be too reluctant to introduce cross-references to other sections or to repeat an essential item of information in a way that makes plain that it is a repetition; th.ir books lack adequate signposting. There is perhaps a feeling that it insults the reader's intelligence to remind him of some fact he has already been told, but nobody can be offended by a reminder in ·

brackets especially if the author tactfully acknowledges the fact that it is a reminder. For instance: (As mentioned in chapter 1, adequate signposting is especially useful when a book is aimed at two markets, perhaps helping laymen or young readers to find their way round a technical work.) What does offend or at least puzzle readers is a lack of clarity, and in particular those hazy circular arguments that suddenly bring you back to your starting point.

Disorderly manuscripts will repeat the same facts, the same sentiments, sometimes the same adjectives, perhaps a couple of pages, perhaps thirty-nine pages, apart.

The Number of Drafts

New authors often seem unable to decide whether they are likely to need one or more rough drafts before getting the final manuscript typed, and whether the first attempt should be written or typed. Obviously this is entirely a matter for the individual; the only rule is that the copy sent to the publisher should be neatly typed. For safety's sake, one copy of the manuscript should *always* remain in your possession. You are even better advised to make as many carbon copies as your typewriter can legibly produce. Very few authors indeed, however, can turn out perfect copy in the right order straight from a typewriter they are having to feed with carbons and flimsy sheets as well as with top-copy paper. So there will be a preliminary draft in some form or other.

Typing is for most people quicker and neater, and if you can translate your thoughts to paper via the machine, so much the better; if your writing output becomes sizeable, you will need to do so. Typewriters and dictaphones are of course accepted as routine tools far more readily than in times past; a generation ago many would have thought it shocking to suggest bypassing the physical chore of handwriting, though actually some famous authors did help popularize the typewriter in literary circles at a very early stage.

But everyone has to discover a recipe for himself taking his personal circumstances into account. While some writers often prefer to work quickly through two preliminary drafts, others may prefer to polish a single draft as they go. For most people, though, it pays to leave a gap between writing the first draft and revising it; if the first chapter drafts are written over a period, to compress your revision into a shorter time may produce better continuity; and if the chapters are produced in a different order from that to be used in the book, it is sensible to revise them in the correct order. But necessary and useful though revision is, you can spend too long at it and if you interfere with your original work (especially your basic factual structure) too much, you may rob it of spontaneity. Whether you write or type the rough draft, it may help to use abbreviations; journalists use a simple t for the, o for of, w for with, tt for that, hv for have, and so on, and leave out vowels in many longer words.

If you write or type on the same standard-sized paper, you can know roughly how many words that sheet accommodates. Many books have to be written to a specified length, and the author who values his time will allocate a rough length to each chapter and make sure that he does not grossly exceed or fall short of it. Up to 10 or 15 per cent of your words may then be lost in polishing and revision without the deletion of actual factual material. Indeed many of the best books are those that have had to be slightly shortened after first writing so that all repetitions and superfluous words are removed. Do not be stingy in supplying yourself with suitable paper. If your time is worth anything at all, it will not pay to use miscellaneous scraps which are hard to file tidily and prevent easy assessment of length.

Typewriters and Tape Recorders

Whether or not you type the rough draft, or indeed even if you have the final copy for the publisher prepared by a professional typist, you will find a typewriter essential. It can be invaluable for notemaking in research; your business letters, including those to your publisher, will look far more professional when your typist may not be available, and you can retype any odd sheets altered after the main typing has been completed. The author who says that he cannot afford to buy, or cannot be bothered to learn to use, a simple portable typewriter has just not arrived. Yet one still comes across engineers and others regularly using advanced equipment in their everyday jobs who fight shy of the typewriter. Anyone who can drive a car, take photographs or even use a vacuum cleaner should be able to master a typewriter using two or four fingers in amateur style within a matter of hours—and even with two fingers a speed much exceeding that of most people's handwriting can quickly be acquired.

One of the larger, more robust portable models at around $100 should, with reasonable care, outlive several cars at over thirty times the price, and there are tax savings (see chapter 8). Whether or not you give the machine regular mechanical attention, do not be niggardly over ribbon changes (unless you specifically need the second color, all-black ribbons of course give best value) and occasionally clean the keys or at least remove the accumulations of dirt which "fill in" letters such as e, a, and o.

If your typist retypes your manuscript in final form at the same time as you want to compose fresh copy or write letters or notes, then it is not ludicrous extravagance to buy a second machine, perhaps second-hand. Writing a book is often hard enough without rendering the mechanics unneccessarily difficult. (To quote another example, some authors are continually interrupted by telephone calls for their wives or children having to be taken in the work room, yet do not feel justified in moving the telephone or adding an extension which might cost the equivalent of time spent in producing only half a dozen pages of good copy.)

Many people do not find tape recorders and other recording gadgets so useful, partly because it is genuinely difficult to dictate long continuous passages smoothly while keeping to the point and partly because it is harder to revise and inject new material into what you have said. But some authors find it easiest to break the ice in this way—to get their matter spoken roughly on to tape, then typed, and then revised. Certainly a dictating machine has its uses in research.

Points of English

Firstly, most people who consider writing a book at all probably know how to write in some kind of style; they may not completely have forgotten their school English; they will at the very least be used to writing letters. And if they want help there are specialist works on the market.

Secondly, from the publication point of view it curiously matters much less if a writer's English is unpolished than if he cannot sort out his subject range and order of ingredients. Consider the publisher's position. Few of his staff or freelance editors are skilled enough to tear apart a disorderly manuscript on a complicated subject and restore it so that if flows as sweetly as though it had been written with the correct progression of material in the first place. The cost of this skilled work, even if someone can be found to do it, is such that manuscripts needing drastic replanning usually have to be rejected. Compared with that, it is simple enough for a copyeditor to smooth out grammar and clumsy sentences and even to rewrite complete paragraphs, providing the basic planning of the book is satisfactory.

This book is not of course for authors who hope to write literary classics. Most of those writing factual books, using language simply as a tool with which to present the material, should merely do their best. That is not to say that skilled use of language is not important; some strictly factual books are so well written that they are works of pure literature in their own right, and they serve their subject all the better for it. But if your book is full of interesting material, logically presented, a polished command of language is not essential, especially if you find a publisher who sees the virtue of the work as a whole and is prepared to help in giving the final polish.

If there is a hint more useful than all others it is that good writers are those who read widely. If a book can earn the comment "A well thought-out synthesis resulting from careful research" the author has become a professional. Reading is obviously the essence of research; but it is equally the basis of being able to synthesize, to present a smooth, rounded treatment with good perspective and the wood standing out firmly from the trees. For reading not only teaches the basic facts you need to know about your subject, but the broader background—and of course how to handle the English language with an adequate vocabulary and variety of construction.

Especially if you are a technically-minded person with something to communicate rather than the desire to communicate for its own sake, extend your reading to subjects other than your own. Whether it is a newspaper or a novel, whether you read yourself or your wife reads to you, or you listen to the radio—imbibe, note how other people communicate, get yourself interested in the whole business of conveying fact and argument through the written word.

Your style of writing will be your own. "Rules" do not matter, but commonsense does. You will, for instance, realize that not everything you have to say is of equal importance, and will seek to develop high spots standing out above the more ordinary parts of the book. As in music, an unvaried pitch or tone becomes tedious. Much can be achieved by careful variation in the length of sentences, using simple ones with a single phrase and more complex ones with several associated statements. Any competent writer avoids overworking a particular construction and especially any personal trick of style; neither diehard traditionalists, writing in nineteenth-century style and employing archaic constructions and phrases, nor pace-setters eager to turn fresh nouns into verbs are easy or convincing to read. Especially on new and technical subjects, a fairly modern style is usually the happiest, adopting some of the contemporary conventions, even at the expense of some of the older grammatical rules, but never relying on jargon or extreme

47

colloquialism.

To have your work read aloud by someone else is a severe but invaluable test; it is the nearest you can get to receiving your message as others will, for familiarity with the written words tends to impair your own impartiality. Once something has been written at all, if it is passable English, it may be taken too much for granted that the words used are the best and that the arguments are convincing. Reading aloud can cruelly show up weak continuity and weak writing.

4

THE PHYSICAL BOOK

THE PHYSICAL BOOK

Technical Limitations

Many authors would enjoy their work more, and have better relations with their publishers, if they appreciated even a little about the technical limitations of book production, which from many points of view is still a depressingly rough-and-ready process. For those wanting greater detail on printing, binding, illustrations, etcetera, there are specialist works available. Here the aspects of production immediately relevant to the writer are discussed; this is where his own influence for good or bad will be most felt by the publisher and printer. At the beginning, when you consider what your finished book will look like and those who will buy it, it helps to bear in mind a couple of well-proven facts that publishers and booksellers have to live with.

Perhaps the most difficult to credit is that a large proportion of the book-buying public judge value for money partly in terms of physical bulk, especially the book's thickness. That this should be so in an age of small homes and limited shelf room is perhaps as surprising as it is regrettable, but it is undeniably true. Increasingly book-buyers are prepared to pay a good price for a specialist work with reference value, but with very few exceptions (such as the ultra-technical manual) this price has to be backed up by physical bulk. Purchasers have to be made to feel justified in spending their money, and that an expensive work must be dressed up to look like one. So the fact that a book with 350 well-filled pages represents good value at a certain price is unfortunately not recognized if the paper is so thin (no matter how high the quality) that the physical bulk is less than that of many books of 200 pages.

If this sounds absurd, make sure that you yourself do not sometimes take the same line, being shocked by the high price of a book that appears smaller than it is.

Remember, too, that the publisher has first to sell books to booksellers. If the booksellers feel they look too small for their price, copies may never reach bookshop shelves in quantities adequate to insure a good initial circulation. And even if the specialist reader feels that a book represents good value, he may—in practice—have to justify the expenditure. It goes against the grain to pay more for an article than it appears to be worth. A professor once gave his wife the price of a book he required urgently and which she offered to buy while in town shopping; though she knew the need for the work and its price, she was unprepared for what struck her as its bad value since it was printed on thin paper and—unable to bring herself to make the purchase—sheepishly went home without it.

Many authors will say that all this is ridiculous. Perhaps most of us in the trade have felt like that ourselves at some time. But experience proves that there is virtually only one exception to the rule about bulk or thickness: with picture books printed on high-class art paper, which does not bulk much but weighs a lot, people are prepared to judge value for money on a weight basis instead! Otherwise only extremely technical works are exempt: manuals bought simply as essential tools, books that would have to be bought whatever the price and format.

Throughout the trade people expect hardbacks to be expensive and paperbacks to be cheap, and they expect all but the most popular new books, those that will sell in tens of thousands, first to appear as hardbacks, to enable their publishers to recoup the costs of typesetting and platemaking quickly, and to enable their authors to gain a fair return. Paperback sales must be regarded as the extras earned by successful books. Sometimes certain types of book are published simultaneously as hardbacks and paperbacks, but even so the paperback sales should be regarded largely as extra ones—for in fact public libraries and other institutions, and also many private buyers, will still prefer the hardback form with its greater durability.

A separate word should perhaps be said about educational books. Many are produced exclusively for classroom use, and may be produced in paperback form (in very large numbers of course) or as hardbacks using cheap materials and without jackets. But the boundary between educational and non-educational books is becoming blurred; many works written as school texts eventually having a general sale in a conventional "trade" edition at a higher price. The author will receive far more royalty per copy from the trade edition than from the educational one.

Some publishers might decide to publish your book in paperback form in the first instance. In this case the first printing would be minimally 5,000 to 10,000 copies.

Additionally, there are several "mass market" paperback publishing houses which have taken to producing some paperback originals (pocket-sized, slick-cover books). They may publish your book if they think it has sufficient appeal for a 25,000 to 40,000 first printing; these books normally sell for one dollar. Generally, as previously stated, books on specific academic subjects do not fall into this category. But for the few exceptions, you might decide to try this route by submitting your manuscript to a "mass market" publisher as a paperback original. If successful, you will be communicating with a much wider audience, and, after all, this *is* one of the names of the game. On the other side of the coin your book will be automatically ignored by the major reviewers throughout the country merely because of its paperback format; there is no sound intellectual reason for this and hopefully the situation will be remedied one day. Secondly, your royalty return will be half (percentage-wise) of the royalty you receive from a hardback edition. Lastly, your work will appear in a cheap and nondescript graphic form. In selecting a publisher (more fully discussed in a succeeding chapter) this first decision of a paperback versus a hardback publisher will be yours alone.

Illustrations

Most authors of non-fiction books like to illustrate their work with photographs, sketches, etc. Sometimes, one picture is indeed worth a thousand words. But it might be helpful here to explain in detail the truly impossible economics of publishing so that you will understand what appears to be a frugal attitude on the publisher's part when he considers your manuscript.

If a book retails at $10, the bookseller and wholesaler receive an average discount of 38% or $3.80, and the author, $1 (minimally) as royalty. Of the $5.20 balance, approximately $2 is spent in actually manufacturing the book, 70c will be consumed by the cost of advertising and selling it, and 30c is the cost for shipping and warehousing. In addition to the normal overhead which the publisher has such as rent, utilities and payroll, he has editorial costs. On average, these expenses can consume the remaining amount. Without accounting for profit (an impossibility, since the combined costs have already utilized 100% of the original $10), mention has not been made of free copies to reviewers, etc. The bedeviled publisher may, therefore, look askance at your bulging folders of illustrations when you insist that your photographs must appear in full color.

The cost of reproducing photographs (half-tones) is many times the cost of reproducing type. So, unless this is to be an art or photographic book, try to keep your illustrations to a minimum.

54

Other Cost Considerations for Illustrations

Curiously, though buyers of many kinds of non-fiction book₅ expect a fair modicum of illustrations, they are not necessarily prepared to pay more for a large number. In the assessment of a book's value, plate pages frequently seem to be regarded as an optional extra—there must be a reasonable minimum, but anything above that tends not to be taken into account. So the publisher may offer the author the use of up to 16 pages of plates but remain reluctant to go further, since he might not safely be able to raise the book's price to cover 24, 32 or 48 pages.

There are probably several reasons why the plates tend to be disregarded in the value for money assessment. The plate pages themselves add little to the bulk of a book. For instance, another 64 pages of plates in this book would make it surprisingly little thicker, and if the price were doubled (as it would probably have to be, to cover the high costs of plates, art paper and plate printing) it would appear poor value. And usually plate pages are not numbered in consecutively with the text pages. In the heading of most book reviews, the number of pages will be quoted along with the title, but this is the highest folio number to be found—the number of the last page. It usually excludes the plates, and if the number of plate pages is high in relation to the number of text pages, the yardstick is obviously misleading. Today some publishers arrange one consecutive numbering sequence throughout their books, taking in front matter pages, the main text, plate pages and all. (Next time you look to see how many pages a book has, check whether the front matter pages have a separate sequence in Roman numerals, which can be useful from the publisher's point of view if the number of pages needed for the front matter is not known when the main text is paginated; and check whether any half-tone pages are included in the main sequence. For short books, publishers often prefer to add all the page numbers together to produce the highest possible total.)

Although buyers are often unwilling to take them into account when assessing the value for money offered by a book, the photographs are the most costly ingredient. The plates from which they are printed, the art paper, and the binding of the special plate pages may combine to make these picture pages several times as expensive as the text ones. Their number must therefore be limited. If it appears that the subject cannot be covered satisfactorily without a very large number of photographs, the only solution may be to produce a "picture book," with large pages printed on art paper throughout, or to run a picture book in parallel with the volume of text, which might then have only a few illustrations.

Line illustrations that can be printed on the text pages are a much easier proposition, at least providing there is no expensive drawing work involved. The necessary plates are cheaper to make and can be printed at no greater cost than type on the ordinary text pages. And the use of these extra pages of ordinary, bulkier paper will make the book bigger and better value. Added to all that, they are still illustrations! So publishers who have to be mean in the allocation of plate pages are often generous in accommodating line drawings. The only line work that a publisher avoids whenever he can is folding maps and plans. These have to be printed separately and often folded, as well as tipped-in to the book, by expensive hand labor. They give poor value for money and again tend not to be taken into account by buyers assessing a book's value. Usually it will be cheaper to have three or four separate line illustrations on the pages of a book, each perhaps going across two pages, than a single folding plan. Printing a map on the book pages of course limits its size, but judicious use can be made of double-page spreads in the middle of 16-page sections. Ideally maps for double-page spreads need drawing with as little detail down the middle as possible; some material tends to disappear in the central gutter.

Details of the kinds of pictures that can be used as line

illustrations on text pages, and those that must be reproduced as half-tones on plate pages, are given in chapter 5.

Color pictures should also be mentioned. Lithography and gravure enable popular books with substantial print runs to carry many color pictures, often at comparatively low published prices—especially low if an international "hook-up" between publishers has been possible and the pictures for books whose texts may later be printed in various languages are all machined in one operation. But for an offset book with a first print order in the 3,500 range, full color reproductions are not a practical proposition.

The only place where color is usually commercially justified is on the jacket. Having made a color plate for the jacket, many publishers are willing to use it a second time to provide a frontispiece. The identical picture, will be used, (often better produced than on the jacket), on real art paper and given a caption. To secure maximum economy, some publishers print the color plates from a number of book jackets all together on the same sheet of art paper which is then split up to form the frontispieces for the various books—perhaps each of them otherwise printed by a different printer. To justify further color plates in a semi-specialist or specialist non-fiction book printed by letterpress is often difficult. Even if another three pages of color are added, at a cost that must be reflected in the published price, they still scarcely make a splash. The few color pictures may indeed merely emphasize the lack of color in the majority of the book, spoiling the impact of excellent black-and-white photographs.

Binding and Jacket

Few buyers notice if the publisher of a hardback book spends extra money on real instead of imitation cloth, or on more or better typography.

The jacket is the last, but still a vitally important, part of the physical book. Many authors are surprised to learn that it is the first part to be produced by some publishing houses. Its early emergence is for publicity purposes: the publisher's representatives solicit orders from booksellers by showing it, and public library suppliers circulate their customers with advance copies.

Originally the jacket, a fairly modern innovation in the history of books, was genuinely a "dustcover" designed merely to protect the binding. Today its publicity and sales function is far more important than its protective one, though it must still be strong enough not to be torn on booksellers' shelves. The jacket will probably have an illustration which must be chosen with great care. It might be informative as well as eye-catching, with its blurb describing the book's basic aims and achievements, with perhaps a note about the author. The jacket can be almost a miniature magazine and is certainly costly to produce.

Authors are seldom consulted about the jacket design, the size or the format of the book. Publishers have their own designers perform this function. Suggestions or insistence by the author in these areas are regarded as troublesome. It would be preferable to refrain from offering this kind of advice unless asked.

Considerable experience is needed actually to design a successful jacket; indeed, talk about jackets accounts for much conversation among publishers and their sales representatives. A good jacket, attractive, compelling, but above all giving the right indication of the book's character, produced and circulated punctually (which may mean three months ahead of publication) can take the book halfway to success, while many an excellent work has been killed by a bad or unsuitable jacket.

Increasingly public libraries find jackets so useful, attractive and informative that they fix them permanently in position around the book, even if the book has been rebound to give it extra strength for library use. Since the jacket's flaps wrap round the inside of the binding case, they obliterate part of any endpaper map or decoration the book may have. Covering up a decoration does not matter unduly, but blotting out part of a map or diagram essential to the understanding of the book certainly does. Endpaper maps have long been unpopular with libraries, but today more than ever should be avoided—unless the map can be repeated within the book where it will not be partly obliterated.

5

YOUR MANUSCRIPT

YOUR MANUSCRIPT

Make it Easy to Read and Handle

However much a publisher may love books (and most of them are in the book business because they do), he rarely enjoys handling the actual manuscript. At best it will be taken for granted, the presentation not impeding the absorption of the words. At worst it will cause infinite frustration, making intelligent reading nigh impossible; the reader may even start by cutting a finger with some gruesome metal fastening in one of those ferociously complicated binders that inexperienced authors occasionally seek out.

A typewritten page starts by being larger than the page of a conventional book, and any extra encumbrance such as an elaborate binder adds unnecessarily to size and weight. Manuscripts have to be mailed to members of the staff, carried home in briefcases, read late in the evenings and even in bed, consulted in cars and on trains: keep their sheer physical bulk to the minimum. Avoid the elaborate binder that may be useful for storing work intended to be consulted only occasionally. Ring binders are especially unpopular since the publisher cannot easily discard them—or if he does take the manuscript pages off the ring, they may take a considerable time to thread back neatly. A petty enough objection—but to someone working under pressure and handling pieces of manuscript all day, a battle with the mechanics can be the last straw. A loose manuscript without any kind of binding or fastening except for big paperclips holding together the pages of each individual chapter is preferable. The ideal container is nothing more elaborate than the box in which the typing paper was bought.

At present most publishers and printers prefer 8-1/2 x 11 inch sheets. Larger sizes such as foolscap should be avoided, since they are less convenient to handle, whether they are being read by the publisher in bed on Sunday morning or set by the printer on a monotype machine (where the foolscap sheet usually has to be folded in two while the standard size can be visible all at one time). Certainly keep to the same-sized paper and typing throughout, and always type in full double spacing, leaving ample margins at top and bottom and a clear one and a half inches down the left. The more even the typing and margins, the easier it will be to "cast off" the manuscript (estimate its length).

A reasonable number of clear handwritten corrections or crossings-out do not matter. Your manuscript should not seek to be a prize exhibit for a show, but merely to be businesslike and clear in all its details. If you must make more changes than can be comfortably accommodated between the typed lines or in the margins, retype a portion and paste it over the appropriate part of the original. If the new version is longer than the old, or whenever substantial additional material has to be injected midway down a page, the original sheet should be cut right across, the new matter being pasted or taped on to it in the correct position; any lines displaced at the bottom of the original sheet should then be pasted to a fresh sheet of the same size; however few lines of copy this holds it should then be numbered into the sequence. This system insures that the printer is presented with material in the right order on pages all of the same size, and is not expected to take in copy on a second sheet while he is midway down the first sheet—a time-wasting process, with the risk that the operator will forget to go back and complete the first page. Never stick or staple small pieces of paper to the edge of the manuscript.

The manuscript pages should of course be numbered consecutively throughout. We say "of course," but many authors still present their work without any page numbers whatsoever, or with the numbers beginning afresh at 1 for each chapter. Consecutive numbering throughout is not mere ritual: it enables the publisher to make an intelligent guess at the book's overall number of words without having to count the pages individually or add up the numbers of pages in the individual chapters; and enables him confidently to detach pages from the manuscript for closer study, perhaps to compare the contents of one section with another, without the nightmare possibility of creating an unsortable muddle. If additional sheets are added after the numbering has been done, they should carry the same numbers as the previous sheets plus a, b, c, etc. If one of the original sheets ceases to exist after deletions have been made, indicate "no number 32" or mark page 31 "31-2" so that printer or publisher quickly sees what has happened.

A table of contents with the manuscript-page numbers marked in pencil can usefully help the publisher or his reader find his way round; but do not type in the numbers, since obviously they will not correspond with the ultimate printed-page numbers. Similarly, within your text it can help to add in pencil the numbers of manuscript pages referred to, while typing XX to indicate to the printer that the correct printed page number will be supplied in proof.

The top copy of the manuscript should be on good-quality typing paper that will stand fair wear and tear. Type as many carbon copies as your typewriter will legibly produce. One of the copies should be retained by the author for safety's sake in case of loss in the mail or fire in the publisher's office; but the publisher may also request a copy, or be pleased to receive one without requesting it, so that he can get the book estimated by a printer while the top copy is being copyedited, and later can

64

have a copy by him in the office when the top manuscript is with the printer or perhaps send one to an overseas publisher for sale of foreign rights.

All corrections and changes, including changes in pagination, should be carefully made on all copies so that they exactly tally. Many a muddle could have been avoided had the author taken the trouble to renumber the carbon copy he retained when renumbering the top copy dispatched to the publisher.

The publisher will give basic instructions to the printer, but an author can help by indicating, for instance, any special deviations from the standard house style and any possible elasticity in the placing of tables, or the layout of awkward quotations. Directions to the printer should ideally be written in a different colored ink or begin with a bold PRINTER so that the comment does not look like part of the manuscript itself. As will be seen in the next chapter, the position of line illustrations should also be boldly marked in the margins.

The Final Preparation

The manuscript should be finished off as though it were in fact the first proof. If it is so untidy that you cannot trust your own checking, retype the troublesome pages. The cost of retyping will be negligible compared with that of making changes once the work is set up in type. If a situation described in your book is changing rapidly, emphasize the difficulty to your publisher and try to arrange to have the manuscript back to make essential last-minute changes just before it gets committed to type. If the proofs then follow within a couple of months, few further changes should be needed.

Mark clearly where all "extract" matter such as quotations and tables is to go, whether quotations are to be indented and put in smaller type, where line illustrations are to be placed and with what captions, and decide on your system of headings and subheadings. Insert all footnotes accurately. If you prepare your final manuscript meticulously you will fail to understand why some other authors find proof-reading such a headache. And your publisher will love you.

Although you will have marked on the manuscript the positions for all drawings, maps and diagrams to appear on the text pages, do not include the illustrations themselves; these should be placed in a separate folder, with their captions and with a clear numbering sequence of their own and cross-referencing to the manuscript page numbers concerned. Photographs and their captions should be placed in another separate folder (see chapter 5).

Headings and Notes

Chapter headings should be clearly indicated at the beginning of each chapter of the manuscript, and so far as the subject allows should be of roughly the same length for all chapters in the book. It helps to make them reasonably short since they may be used as the running head at the top of the right-hand pages. However, in order to cut costs, some publishers eliminate running heads altogether.

Decide whether or not you need subheadings and work out a consistent scheme which can be applied to the book as a whole. The actual typography or layout will be decided by the publisher, but make clear the relative *weight* or importance of each heading. For instance, the main chapter title can be typed in upper and lower case (small letters except for a capital initial letter for important words); the main section headings should then be centered in block capitals; a third category of heading, to mark divisions within the material covered by the main section or subheading, could then be placed at the side in upper and lower case and underlined to appear in italics. In addition, you can indicate the relative weight by placing a letter beside the headings—A for the full chapter heading, B for the main section or subheading, C for the side heading, and even D if yet another division is necessary. Lack of clarity and consistency can cause untold confusion, not only to the publisher, editor and typesetter, but (if they do not correct matters) to the book's readers.

Notes and references must also be treated consistently. What notes are needed and why? Differentiate in your mind between the note that elaborates on a particular point or gives additional information, and the reference which merely quotes the source of information. Both kinds may be placed at the foot of the page, or both kinds consolidated at the end of the book, or you can rationally place a relatively small number of genuine notes at the foot of the page while having the source references at the back of the book. If the notes are to appear at the foot of the page, type them immediately after the line to which they refer, but rule them off from the ordinary text. If they are to appear at the end of the book, of course type them in sequence on separate sheets.

Where notes are consolidated at the end of the book (the cheaper and often the tidier method), they are normally numbered from 1 up consecutively, starting a new sequence for each chapter. Raised index numbers are inserted on the text page in the relevant positions, preferably at the end of a sentence. Any footnotes actually appearing on the text pages are normally indicated by symbols: the first by an asterisk *, the second by a dagger †. A single note at the foot of the last page of each chapter can indicate the page number (to be completed in proof) on which that chapter's notes will be found; and in the notes section at the back you can quote the number and title of each chapter and indicate which text pages it occupies. This simple cross-referencing largely overcomes the objection that notes at the back of the book are inconvenient to use. Remember that there is a two-way traffic between text and notes, for some people may read the notes for their own interest and want to refer readily back to the text.

If you are writing a book for the general public, it is recommended that a large number of footnotes be placed at the end of the book. This will make the reading easier and uninterrupted. Footnotes on each page are acceptable, however, for the academic book which will be read by professionals (textbook). In the latter case, number them starting at 1 for each chapter. Never number notes consecutively throughout a complete book in either case. Should there be a single addition or deletion in editing or for any other reason, all those that follow will need renumbering.

Even in the academic book it is often possible to avoid notes altogether by making simple explanations or citing sources in brackets; (Smith, David, 1969) adequately refers the reader to the full entry in the bibliography (*Industrial Britain: The North West*, 1969). Simply to explain "As David Smith has said" is perhaps the most readable approach when your book is intended partly for readers unused to the conventions of academic books.

The way in which book titles, and titles of journals and articles, should be printed in notes and citations as well as in the bibliography is stated in the note on bibliographies in the back-matter section of this chapter. Where full details of a book, journal or other material are given in the bibliography, an abbreviated version is adequate for the notes; and when a particular source is cited repeatedly, again use an abbreviated version for each reference after the first. This is more helpful to the reader than to use the old-fashioned *op cit* or *ibid*.

Style

Authors should also seek consistency in smaller details such as the capitalization and spelling of words, punctuation and the use of abbreviations.

Where no particular publisher is in mind, all that matters is that the style is uniform—that if double quotation marks are used on the first page they are used consistently throughout (quotations within quotations being in single quote marks), that feet and inches are not spelled out in full on one line, abbreviated as ft and ins on the next and as ft. and in. on the third. Stick to the Chairman or the chairman (where there is doubt normally the capital is dropped these days), m.p.h., mph or miles per hour. Where you are employing a typist to prepare the final manuscript, make sure that she knows what is wanted.

Occasionally a publisher accepts a manuscript whose content had some shortcomings because it was beautifully typed and consistently presented in style, chapter headings, note arrangements, etc.; this part of the editorial savings to the publisher was probably applied to strengthening the basic text.

Frontmatter

A careful author supplies copy for the frontmatter pages, and for the backmatter. Each page should be typed on a separate sheet of paper. The frontmatter is normally made up as follows:

Half-title page This merely carries the book's main title, typed on an otherwise blank sheet of copy paper.

Half-title verso "Verso" means left-hand page. The page at the back of the half-title is sometimes left blank, but if the author wishes to list his previous books he should do so on the sheet representing this page. ("Recto" refers to right-hand pages.)

Title page The author can set out the title, sub-title if any, his name and any degrees or qualifications he thinks relevant enough to display and the publisher's name.

Title verso The information on this page will be supplied by the publisher at a later date and is no concern of the author at this time. It deals with copyright, Standard Book Number, Library of Congress Catalogue Card number, etc.

Dedication If there is to be a dedication or quotation, this should follow next. The publisher should have it at the start so that he can provide for it when the manuscript is cast off. (A cast off is a determination of the amount of pages the book will have when typeset.) Especially if to save pages would help to produce an even printing working, a short dedication or quotation is sometimes accommodated on the title verso. If however it is given the prominence of the right-hand page opposite the title verso then the page that follows it (normally the sixth text page in the book) will be blank.

Table of contents   The author can set this out by following the style adopted by a table of contents in a book of a similar kind. If chapters are broken into sections with subheadings, each subheading may be listed under the chapter title as is done in this book. As hinted earlier, it helps the publisher find his way around a manuscript if the manuscript-page numbers can be inserted in pencil, the final printed-page numbers of course having to wait until the book is in page proof.

List of illustrations   Again the author can provide it, by following the style of the list in a similar book. Fairly abbreviated captions are given here, though sometimes the list also acknowledges the sources of the illustrations. Acknowledgment of illustrations may be on a separate page in the front matter, or a paragraph on the copyright page, or in the back of the book. Half-tones are usually listed first and then line illustrations in a second sequence under a sub-heading "IN THE TEXT;" this is partly because until the book is in page proof you cannot tell where the half-tones and illustrations will fall in relation to each other, making it impossible to provide in advance a single list of all types of illustration in the correct sequence.

Preface/Foreword   This is an optional extra less frequently used than in the past. Today people increasingly like to judge a book themselves on its own merit, and a preface either by the author or by some famous personage he has persuaded to help *sell* the work cuts less ice—or can even arouse a hostile reaction. A simple explanation of how the book came to be written and its aims can sometimes be useful, and the author can also use the preface or foreword to thank those who have helped him. Very rarely is both a preface and a foreword needed in a book of ordinary length and scholarship.

Introduction   If personal acknowledgments are not included and the introduction is an integral part of the book, introducing the subject matter rather than the book itself, this can be numbered as the first chapter; otherwise it is usually

70

outside the chapter sequence.

Acknowledgments Try to keep these down to an essential minimum, and avoid cliches such as thanking your wife for her tact and endurance while the book was written. It is always best to incorporate acknowledgments in the introduction, rather than a separate entity. One word of caution. In an attempt at modesty, either false or otherwise, do not attempt to list your faults and omissions. You might succeed in discouraging the reader at this early point in the manuscript.

Backmatter

Where all or any of the following are to be included, they are placed at the end of the book. The following is the usual order though there is no hard-and-fast rule.

Gazetteer A gazetteer or an amplified geographical list of any kind, supplied as a basic part of the book as distinct from an appendix, is useful when dealing with certain kinds of subjects (such as archaeology) and is normally placed before the end-matter proper.

Notes and references If notes are necessary and are not carried at the foot of each individual page, they normally appear immediately after the close of the continuous text. The notes for each chapter should be presented separately under a sub-heading carrying that chapter's number, title and preferably also text-page numbers to facilitate cross-reference between notes and text.

Appendices As the word implies, these are extras not essential to the understanding of the basic book, and therefore they usually come after the notes documenting or amplifying the chapters. An appendix may provide additional material, such as the complete text of an historic document, a note on research methods, or an example of how things are organized in a different country, or it can repeat information given in the text in a different, often statistical, form. Thus while the text may have dealt with salient points about the dividend record in a company history, an appendix might list the complete dividend performance from the start. Good appendices can give a book an additional dimension, but if the material is thin and suspect it will look even more bogus standing on its own here than incorporated into a chapter. Statistical matter must not of course require more columns than can comfortably be accommodated on the text page or a pair of facing text pages. Publishers are even less likely to agree to folding tables of statistics than to folding maps, since it is usually possible to break down statistical matter into smaller tables, more easily manageable and more comprehensible.

Bibliography Any good non-fiction book needs a bibliography, both to tell the reader where the author found his information and as a signpost to further reading and research material. Indeed, if you have to make a quick judgment on a book, the bibliography is as revealing as any part, and its quality is often mentioned in reviews in learned journals. Bad bibliographies are not only incomplete but lack a rational plan and give inadequate or varying information about the books and other sources listed.

The best plan is to list general works first and then to categorize more specialist works, though sometimes it is easier to list books and other sources individually for each chapter. Guidance about which books and sources proved particularly useful to the author (and might therefore help the reader who wants further information) should be given wherever possible: a list including every conceivable publication on a subject without any hint about its nature or usefulness is usually a waste of space—and certainly do not blindly include references to publications you have not consulted yourself. Perhaps the most useful bibliographies are those with discursive introductions that comment on the main works consulted before printing a formal list. In the formal list, within each category or chapter section, the order of presentation must be consistently alphabetical by author or chronological by original date of publication (preferably the first).

Distinguish carefully between the titles of books and of

chapters in books or articles in journals. Titles of books and of journals should be underlined to appear in italics, while the names of chapters and of articles within these books and journals go in quotation marks and not italics since they are not publications in their own right:

BOOKER, FRANK. *The Industrial Archaeology of the Tamar Valley.* David & Charles, Newton Abbot, 1967.

BOOKER, FRANK. "The Tamar Valley", *Industrial Archaeology,* 1967.

In a book of academic standing the publishers' names should consistently be quoted. Make sure that you refer to the last edition of the books listed.

Index This is the author's responsibility and no one who has written a book to be useful, as distinct from just making money, will lack interest in its quality. It may be necessary to employ someone else (the publisher may find someone on the author's behalf) to do the actual labor of collating the entries and placing them in alphabetical order, but even then the author should give the necessary starting guidance and exercise quality control.

A few books may need two or more indexes, but where possible consolidate all entries into a single sequence. The best indexes are not necessarily the longest and certainly not the most complicated; the aim should be to include all topics *of importance,* making the best use of the space available if this is limited, and on a scale suited to the book concerned. Especially in shortish books whose prices have to be kept low and where the economy of an even printing working is essential, be prepared to make last-minute cuts to fit a smaller space if need be.

A brief note at the head of the index explaining its scope may be useful, and can indicate any particular system adopted, for instance, Congressional Acts are listed under their individual titles, and that page numbers in bold type (indicated on the typescript by wavy underlining) refer to the principal entries or to illustrations as the case may be. If the book is within a series, then follow the general series scope of the index as well as its precise layout.

The index cannot of course be completed until the book is in page proof, but delay at that stage has to be kept to the minimum. So make the framework in advance, from a carbon copy of the manuscript; even if the publisher has asked for the only carbon copy at the start of production, he may be able to return it for index use long before the proofs are due. The most thorough approach is probably to underline on the manuscript all the items you want indexed, and then to build up a card-index system, typing from the cards once they have been checked and arranged in alphabetical order.

Type in double or treble spacing, with wide margins, so that any last-minute changes can be made without loss of legibility—and make at least one carbon. Make abundantly plain which are the main entries, and which are sub-headings under a main one. Use the same styles as elsewhere in the book, though for an index some abbreviations may be necessary; use these consistently. Accurate punctuation is vitally important in an index: normally a comma (or occasionally a colon) is used after the item you are indexing, with a comma after each page number and a semi-colon at the end of each sequence within a composite entry.

Where the book concentrates on one main theme, such as the history of merchant shipping, the life of a statesman, or a particular breed of dog, it is usually sensible to omit any general entry for that subject. A long string of sub-headings is difficult to use, and in any case the reader is likely to look for an entry for the particular aspect he wants. All other important topics must have entries, and where a long string of page numbers accumulates these entries should be subdivided. In the following example, the page numbers immediately following the main heading are indexing the references to Italy as a whole and in general; the subheadings pick out the references to individual aspects. It helps to arrange the subheadings i: alphabetical order.

Italy, 37, 73, 111-13; agriculture, 36-7, 146; architecture,

153-5; history, 2-13, 150-1, 200; industries, 30, 99, 203-10; transport 95-7, 213-15.

When a subject is dealt with more or less continuously on several successive pages, specify the first and last of the sequence: 125-8. When, however, there are only slight and unconnected references, list the page numbers separately 125, 126, 127, 128 or 125ff.

Cross-referencing is useful when tackled with moderation. Where only a few page numbers are concerned, it is better to repeat them under two headings than to send the reader from one entry to another with a *"see"* reference; but where a composite entry with various subheadings is involved, and the reader may not be sure where to look, then help: Pottery, *see* Porcelain; Occupations, *see* Employment. *See also* references at the end of an entry can help establish connections between different subjects, and in particular can be used to send the reader from a general to a particular entry: Metals, 68-9, 114: *see also* Gold (or: *see also* under individual metals).

When the subject is mentioned in a footnote, add *n* to the page number. Illustrations, too, should be indexed, their page numbers appearing at the end of the sequence for the subject concerned and being underlined to denote italic or bold type.

6

THE ILLUSTRATIONS

THE ILLUSTRATIONS

Their Importance

Illustrations are an important ingredient of most nonfiction books and from the production point of view are often the main feature that distinguishes them from novels and makes them more costly. The interest of booksellers, the number of individuals who buy on impulse, the size of the carefully-scrutinized orders from institutions working on tight budgets and the quality of reviews in the press may all substantially depend upon the success with which the author has been able to match his words with his illustrations. Reviewers of nonfiction will often praise the basic text but censure the quality of the maps, or the lack of imagination in the choice of photographs or the poorness of their reproduction.

Most publishers regard illustrations as being basically the responsibility of the author. Not only does the inclusion of the illustration increase the price of the finished book on which the author's royalties are calculated, but the author should be the best judge of how to illustrate his subject and should normally know where the best material is to be found. The publisher should help with both general and technical advice, and sometimes may be able to give specific assistance in finding a particular picture, but the prime responsibility rests with the author. Of course there are well-known authors who refuse pointblank to have anything to do with illustrations, failing to see their potential in strengthening the book as a whole or perhaps knowing that anything they write will sell well enough with minimum attention from them; their publishers may be so pleased to have their books that they accept the position. This book, however, is addressed to the less established writer who may not be able to dictate terms and who in any case will be anxious to build up his subject or his own reputation. Indeed, it is easier for the publisher to undertake the selection of pictures for wide-ranging popular books covering obvious subjects than for the more specialist works with which we are mainly concerned here.

The maximum possible enthusiasm should be brought to the task of finding illustrations. The best collections of photographs are those that have been *selected* from larger collections. Do not examine just enough pictures to fill the space; do not begrudge having to leave out some subject in the final selection, especially if better ones turn up. The discovery of two unpublished historic photographs at the last minute may make all the difference to the interest of the illustrations in the assessment of many readers. Readers are not slow to discover where authors have taken the easiest course, or indeed to discover the weaknesses in a poor map. Conversely, everyone appreciates pictures that not only look good but genuinely complement the text and are well cross-referenced with it.

The biggest mistake is to forget all about illustrations until the writing of the book has been completed. The best selection can probably not be assembled in a hurry: picture agencies, museums and individual photographers often take a considerable time to reply to inquiries, and half a dozen different leads may have to be followed before success is achieved. As soon as you have decided to write a book on a certain subject,

79

open a file for pictures or facts about the whereabouts of known pictures, and initiate inquiries at the earliest opportunity. The final page-by-page arrangement may be best left until the text has been finished, but then it will be too late, for instance, to write a letter for publication in local newspapers asking owners of interesting old photographs on a particular district or subject to let you borrow them for your forthcoming work—often a very productive means of discovering pictures that have not been published before.

As we have seen, from the production point of view there are two main types of illustrations: line illustrations and photographs or half-tones.

Line Illustrations

Unless art paper is used for the whole book, the line illustrations are normally placed on the text pages, and they will be needed by the publisher and the printer simultaneously with the manuscript. They should not however be interleaved with the manuscript but should be sent in a separate folder or envelope since they will first have to go the platemaker, even if they do not need redrawing.

As stated earlier, the line illustrations and the manuscript must be cross-referenced so that the illustrations will be placed correctly in position. Each line illustration should be allotted a number which should be indicated clearly at the appropriate point in the manuscript (preferably in colored ink or crayon to stand out boldly), while the manuscript-page number should also be marked on the illustration. This double check is valuable, since line-illustration material is apt to come in varying shapes and sizes and sometimes has to be packed in more than one container, for instance, envelopes sent with the manuscript and a roll for larger maps.

Remember that your manuscript and illustrations will not be the only ones arriving in the publisher's office by that mail, and the editor concerned will probably not unpack them himself.

Every package should be labeled with the book's title. Make clear how many line illustrations you are mailing, with details of any that are to follow. (So far as possible keep them together.) For safety, perhaps ask the publisher to acknowledge receipt of the number of illustrations sent. It sounds elementary, possibly, but mislaid line illustrations produce more than their fair share of nightmares in publishing offices.

Line illustrations normally fall into two kinds: original source material such as old handbills, engravings and extracts from letters, which will go straight to the platemaker for reproduction; and maps, charts and diagrams which have to be especially drawn or redrawn.

With material already existing, once an illustration is selected as useful for the book concerned, the main considerations are whether it is in fact suitable for the line reproduction process and whether it will reduce satisfactorily in size for accommodation on the book's page.

Line illustrations are, as the term suggests, reproduced entirely by a series of lines. The image is either reproduced in black, or it is not reproduced at all. There is no gradation of tone, as there is in half-tone photographic reproduction, so the line originals must be in sharp black if they are to come out clearly. Old notices were often badly printed and can consist of gradations of greys and actual gaps where no ink was transferred from the type to the page, and therefore they may reproduce patchily, though they can sometimes be touched up before platemaking. Fine hatching or pencil shading may not come out clearly. Old letters normally reproduce well; material from photocopying machines often does not, because it lacks a sharp, clear image, the grey of the printed or written matter sometimes coming out relatively little bolder than the grayish background of the surrounding areas. Send the publisher the original, rather than copied material, whenever possible; good line plates can easily be made from line illustrations in other books, but of course remember copyright considerations. If you have to make copies, try and make them first-class photographs with the black a true black and no background blur. Remember also that if the material is very complicated, trouble may result when the size of the picture has to be reduced for your book: the white gaps between the black lines will "fill in," resulting in a smudgy continuous black.

Turning to maps, charts and diagrams, the author may be able to provide only rough material—material that the publisher's draftsman can follow to produce a professional result. Even if the author is only producing roughs, however, he should bear the page size and shape in mind, try to work to a correct scale (since it will be easier for the draftsman or cartographer to do a straight copy than to establish the basic framework afresh), and make sure he includes everything he wants, with correct spelling (cartographers are human and painstaking, and imagine their reaction when told to change ten names and alter the location of a boundary on their neat maps because the author carelessly fed in the wrong information initially).

The 8 x 5-1/2 inch page can normally accommodate a map of 6 x 4-3/4" less any space that has to be left *underneath* the map for caption. A double-page spread can run to a width of 10 inches with a depth of 8 inches if there is no caption or the caption is fitted into the map area. Normally maps are drawn to a larger scale—often twice the size—then they are reproduced.

Some authors have the ability to produce finished maps ready for the platemaker themselves, and if help can be given in this way the publisher will usually welcome this. Line plates are not costly to make or to print, but professional drawing can be very expensive indeed, so any cost-saving assistance may mean the publisher will accept more maps than might otherwise be possible, or that he will be prepared to give some other concession. Even if the author cannot undertake mapwork himself, he may know a professional geographer, surveyor or someone else who can—and it especially helps if that person has knowledge of the subject matter. The result may well be more purposeful as well as take a shorter time to produce—and if the work is done on a freelance basis and the fee can be paid direct to the cartographer, the cost will almost certainly be very much less than that to the publisher employing a salaried professional on his own staff. But if there is any doubt about your or your colleague's ability to provide the required quality, check carefully after a specimen map or two have been prepared. Often people who can draw good outlines spoil them by shaky or unsuitable lettering, or by unskilled use of stencils, while professional draftsmen sometimes ignore the page size available.

Half-tones

Line subjects   Subjects to be reproduced as line plates must consist entirely of solids, dots or lines with no intermediate gray tones. Tones are simulated by means of dot or line tints.

Half-tone subjects   The half-tone method is used to reproduce any subject which incorporates continuous tone.

As was said earlier, while people expect many kinds of nonfiction books to be well illustrated, they are not normally prepared to pay a higher price for a double ration of pictures. Work realistically within the limitations laid down by the publisher—or the decision reached after bargaining with him. If you have only 16 pages of plates to cover a complicated subject, do not attempt to record everything you can by cramming in numerous small pictures on the page, ignoring all artistic considerations. Most readers do *not* expect to find a complete secondary documentation of the subject in picture form. They look instead for a well-balanced, representative selection, nicely presented, which usually means no more than two pictures to a page, perhaps "bleeding" off the page's edge to make the fullest use of the art paper.

If your subject is one which absolutely demands many pictures, maybe you should be producing a "picture book" on art paper all through. What publishers cannot normally do is provide a full text and as many pictures as in a picture book all for the price of a conventional single volume. Unless the whole work is printed on art paper, your photographs may not appear opposite the text to which they refer, especially in short-run books, which is another reason why good captions (and cross-referencing) are required. But place the pictures so that the progression of subject matter is the same as that in the text, or adopt some other rational progression.

A paragraph of do nots! Do not give your publisher bad pictures of obvious subjects like the Washington Monument, a bus or an animal which any competent photographer can take on any fine day; but a poorer standard is obviously acceptable in the truly historic and irreplaceable picture. Do not submit photographs of vehicles, machines or the like that just cut off outer limits such as the front of the front wheel or the top of a ship's rigging; if you cannot include the whole of the subject, cut part of it away boldy so that it does not look as though you hoped to include the lot and just failed. In a book that could appeal to a wider audience, do not concentrate entirely on close-ups of smaller details without any more general views or shots; the average reader will have less interest in minor details than you have.

Ideally the photographs should be full-plate or at least half-plate size, glossy prints with ample contrast. Pictures to be reproduced in black and white should be taken in black and white in the first place, since whatever satisfaction they may give for family purposes, black-and-white prints off color transparencies are often not good enough for platemaking. Until there is a new technical breakthrough, specialist books are going to be illustrated mainly if not entirely in black and white. Yet today most people take color pictures, and sometimes it is only when publication of a book approaches that it is suddenly realized that enough suitable negatives do not exist.

Label each photograph clearly on the back, and by all means indicate which part of the whole you would like reproduced if some of it is superfluous. Let each picture for each page carry on the back the appropriate page number plus a, b, c, and then add the finishing helpful touch by placing all the photographs for each page in a separate, clearly-labeled envelope. NEVER stick photographs down in an album, or even use a postcard album from which it is difficult to remove and replace pictures speedily, since each picture may have to be handled individually several times during processing.

Though labeling of pictures is vitally important, never write on the photograph itself; marks made on the back can come through and appear on the plates.

Only the reference number should appear on the back of the actual photographs, which the printer will never see. The captions list should be typed on separate sheets.

The same procedures can of course be adopted if the whole book is to be devoted to pictures. Publishers of picture books are pleased to let the author have layout sheets of the right size. Again, few authors will feel capable of doing the precise, finished layout, but basic guidance will help the publisher not only to keep the production costs down but to give the author as near as possible what he wants. The author will know what aspects will particularly interest certain classes of readers, where a large-scale reproduction of detail might be most helpful, and so on, whereas publishing staff not expert in the subject concerned are less likely to strike a right balance if left unaided to allocate space for perhaps 150 pictures.

Even in picture books the temptation to include a large number of small reproductions purely for record purposes should be resisted, for almost certainly most buyers and readers will demand generous treatment of the best topics, which may mean devoting whole pages and occasionally even double-page spreads to a single picture. And again, even in picture books try to produce a rational progression of material: the best result will probably be obtained by starting with a synopsis just as for any other book, allocating certain pages or sections to certain subjects.

Paying for the Illustrations

Most publishers expect their authors to clear the copyright of pictures, which may involve the payment of fees to agencies, museums and even colleagues in the profession or hobby. Sometimes publishers make a contribution toward the fees that authors have to pay. In any event, you will usually find this defined clearly in the contract. As a rule, most publishers require that any cost of illustrations be borne by the author, and further, the author indemnify the publisher in case of copyright infringement in this regard.

Having to foot the bill will make the author budget-conscious, and certainly too much can be paid for permission to use pictures. But, if a publisher has provided a lump sum for picture copyrights, it is shortsighted to attempt to make a profit by retaining some of it: as we have said, the illustrations should be an integral part of a non-fiction book and its standing and sales may be affected by their quality. By all means argue with institutions about the size of their fees and seek reductions; but try to get the best.

Getting the best probably means not using exclusively your own pictures, but if you (or your wife or husband) can provide a proportion, so much the better. Writing a book is a lonely trail not only for the writer but for the partner not actively involved. If you are lucky enough to have a wife or husband who can handle the photographs, taking them him or herself or doing the research and dealing with agencies and museums, it turns the project into a team affair and also has useful tax advantages. But bad photographs or maps are still bad even if the work of your sweetheart; make sure she, or he, can do the job before embarrassing everyone, including the publisher.

$20 or more usually has to be paid to an institution or agency for the use of a single picture, but a reduction can often be negotiated if a dozen or more are chosen at the same time. If you pick a substantial number from the same source, ask if you can delay payment until the book's publication, when you may be receiving the balance of your advance from the publisher. Friends and colleagues are usually more modest in their financial demands and might be content with an acknowledgment and a free copy. But it will be your task, and not the publisher's, to provide the complimentary copy, and if it is to be an expensive book this may prove more costly than paying a fee.

Photographs are protected by copyright. The photographer owns the copyright of his work for 28 years; this is renewable for an additional 28 years. Sometimes, during the second renewal period, the photographer may request Congress to renew his copyright even further. Be certain that whatever material you wish to use has officially gone into the public domain. You may get this information from the Library of Congress in Washington, D. C. But do not be put off using an interesting old picture if you genuinely cannot tell the date of original publication or trace the copyright owner; some postcards, for instance, could have been published equally well in 1915 or 1925, and their publishers have gone out of business. In such cases be prepared to pay a fee should you be asked for one after your book has been published. Maps and artistic work enjoy the same copyright protection as photographs. You do not avoid copyright liability by merely re-lettering or slightly amending someone else's basic work. However, if any material whether illustrative or textual, was originally produced by a United States government agency, it is available for use without requesting permission, except in rare cases where it was printed privately. All works available from the U.S. Government Printing Office bear no copyright. However, you would be well advised to credit that agency with the work somewhere in your book; it will add to the credibility and authority of your manuscript.

YOUR PUBLISHER

7

YOUR PUBLISHER

The Choice of Firm

Publishers' performances differ sharply. Some firms prefer a quick return while others aim at long-term continuing sales. Some take little care with the physical production standards of their books while others always use the best materials and good designers. There are great differences in the approaches to aspects like publicity and the sales of subsidiary rights. One of the biggest contrasts is perhaps in the time that various firms take to convert a manuscript into a completed book.

Perhaps "The Choice of Firm" is a totally incorrect heading for this section. In actual practice, a new author never chooses a publishing firm; rather, after exposing his manuscript to several publishers, a firm will choose him. In spite of the fact that this country is now producing over 35,000 new titles annually, and in spite of the fact that many wonder why much of it is published at all, it is still very difficult to get published. Authors of a dozen published works still get initial rejections on their thirteenth manuscript. So we really refer here to choosing *prospective* publishers.

In practice it is difficult to judge one firm's total performance against another's, to choose the publisher most suitable for your book in every respect, even if the perfect firm does in fact exist. The publishing scene is complex and firms are continually changing their character and their staffs; what would have been good guidance for particular kinds of books ten years ago might be irrelevant today.

You can undertake some simple market research to avoid the worst pitfalls and waste of time. First, find out which publishers handle the kind of book you have written or plan to write. Unless you already know something about publishing, the best starting point will be the list of publishers in *Literary Market Place*, which gives a brief description of the main types of book accepted. Unfortunately firms do not always keep their entries up to date, but at least make sure that you use the latest issue of the *Literary Market Place*.

Send for the catalogues of likely-sounding firms and assess whether your book would look at home there (and check that the same firm has not already published a very similar kind of book too closely duplicating yours for the two to be viable under the same imprint). Go to your library or bookshop to see the books published by an individual publisher you have shortlisted and compare them with books on the same subject issued by other publishers. Or subscribe to *The New York Times Book Review* section for a time and follow the many weekly advertisements of publishers' announcements. Study book reviews, especially in specialist magazines and learned journals covering your subject, noting the publishers and any praise or criticism of production standards and other aspects for which the publisher may have been directly responsible.

You need also to clarify your personal objectives. For instance, if your main aim is to produce a standard work that will enhance your prestige in your profession, the last thing you may want is a short period of high-pressure sales followed by the book being seen sold off cheaply on the bargain counters of bookstores—so pick a publisher sympathetic to academic authors and one with a good record of keeping books alive through successive editions. Conversely, if your main interest is a quick financial return with a substantial advance against royalties, you will probably get it more easily from a large firm in a conglomerate than from a smaller, "closed" company.

Two of the points of greatest importance are unfortunately the hardest to check from outside. Many authors feel it is vital to know roughly how long a publisher will take to convert a manuscript into a finished book. While most firms seldom need more than twelve months or so, some habitually take two years and one can hear of a five-year gap between delivery of manuscript and publication. Then, the matter of subsidiary rights and export sales is more important than new authors may immediately realize, since the publisher really on the ball might be able to double or treble the income from ordinary royalties by selling translation, paperback, serialization and other rights. If you cannot make inquiries on these points first, certainly you should raise them with the publisher once you have approached him and he has expressed an interest in your work.

If the first publisher consulted expresses interest in publishing the manuscript much as it stands, but does not satisfy you in some respect, you take a gamble by turning to another. But presuming that your demands are reasonable, taking into account the sales potential of the manuscript concerned, the risk of doing so will not usually be great; if one house has offered to publish a book, the manuscript is presumably basically publishable.

The question has oftimes come up as to whether or not an author should submit his manuscript to multiple publishers, i.e. to more than one publisher at a time. Actually this practice is becoming more and more prevalent. As an ethical consideration, however, the writer should notify the publishers involved that they are handling such a multiple submission. Some publishers do not care to enter into an "auction" type of competition for a manuscript; others just refuse to do so on principle. In any event, the publisher should have the option in the first instance because publishers send qualified manuscripts out for expensive reading reports and they do not want to learn of a multiple submission after the fact. Actually, it is often in the publisher's best interests to have the work submitted to more than one house because in this way they get to see more properties. The author, on the other hand is able to save a lot of time; single submissions take months to be rejected.

But the matter needs looking at in an entirely different light if a publisher accepts your work subject to your shortening, supplementing or changing it in some way, for that means that he does not regard it as publishable in its present form and others may not do so either. The first publisher you pick could be mad, but on the law of averages his advice, being born of experience, will be sound and it should be taken seriously. If you reject his plan to render the work publishable you may well find that some three months later you have to swallow very similar advice from another publisher who initially stood lower in your list of preferences. Publishers are not infallible, as is perhaps demonstrated by the rapid changes of staff and policies in many firms, but for the most part they are professionals and their basic assessments of treatment, length and scale of illustrations are apt to be uncannily similar—and right.

You would be well advised to get some kind of written contractual agreement from the publisher before rearranging or redoing you manuscript according to his wishes. If he should reject the work after you have fulfilled his requirements or if the editor with whom you dealt resigned or was fired, the next publisher may not agree with the first publisher's or editor's suggestions; he may have an altogether different idea. You could be on a merry-go-round for a long time, losing the original intent and scope of your work along the way. If a publisher is serious about your book and about his own modifications, he will offer a contract at this juncture specifying his right to withdraw if you do not fulfill his requirements. At least the publisher has made a moral and hopefully, a financial commitment at this point.

Agents

This is possibly the first part of the book which may be

controversial. Generally speaking, literary agents are less effective for new writers than established ones. Some publishers, some writers, and of course all agents will disagree with this statement. The reasons are both many and obvious. An agent works on speculation, i.e. he is not paid until and unless he is able to secure a signed contract for you. His fee is usually 10% of all earnings on the book (in perpetuity). This will be approximately 1% of the retail price of the book. You can readily see that an agent must work on many manuscripts simultaneously to earn a living. This means that he may not devote as much time as is required to do a thorough job in covering the publishing field for you. Furthermore, it is more practical for him to devote most of his time to what might be a best-seller. He may not devote much time to a book that has limited economic possibilities.

You, on the other hand, will undoubtedly be willing to work very hard to get your book published, considering all the time you expended in writing it. With approximately 1,100 trade publishers in this country, three rejections would not necessarily discourage you; the agent would tend to drop the matter if he did not get quick results.

Agents tend to feel that they have a "scorecard" with publishers. They are afraid of rejections; too many of them might give them a bad reputation for future submissions. This may not be universally true, but many agents suffer from this psychology. Although many successful writers have withstood twenty and thirty rejections before publication, agents have not.

Finally, many agents will frustrate you with silence. Since they are only paid on performance (contract) and not for their time, they naturally cannot keep you constantly informed concerning their activities in behalf of your manuscript. They cannot take the time to tell you weekly or monthly which publisher is looking at your work, which has rejected it and for what reasons, etc. Months go by without any communication. Harassing them will only make matters worse. They will tell you that they are doing the best they can, as indeed they are; but you will feel that there must be *something* you can do. However, their right to work in behalf of your book is exclusive while they

94

have it; should you be fortunate enough to get a contract on your own during this time, your agent would still be entitled to his fee. In this regard, their operation is similar to that of a real estate agent.

There are, of course, advantages to using an agent, but these advantages may not bear fruit for you personally. For example, many writers cannot psychologically bear rejections; if you are that kind of person, the use of an agent will preclude rejections from ever appearing in your mailbox. All dealings are handled between publisher and agent. If you have written a book and for some reason have received favorable inquiry concerning it, from Hollywood or television, you would do well to let an agent negotiate for you with all parties, including the publisher. In this instance the agent will devote a good deal of his time and energy to this project.

Many non-fiction books have subsidiary rights possibilities (serialization, paperback and translation rights, etc.) and an agent, therefore, is potentially useful. But bear in mind that a well informed publisher does not need an author's agent to prod him about subsidiary rights for his own books. The publisher is ever on the lookout to exploit every translation, serial, book club and paperback possibility for your book. It is in his best financial interests to do so.

Finally you will be told that you need an agent to select the appropriate publishers to whom to submit your manuscript, to advise you properly concerning the correct method of submission, and to assist you with counsel when the time comes to negotiate a contract. But really that is what this book is all about. One of the things this book tries to do is to teach you to be your own best agent for your manuscript.

Should you decide to contact an agent, consult *Literary Market Place* published by R. R. Bowker & Company. You may purchase it or find it in your local library. You will discover that most literary agents are in New York City because the seat of the publishing industry is there. If you do not live in New York, your dealings with an agent will probably be confined to the mails and the telephone.

Making the Direct Approach

There is only one golden rule, and that is to remember that publishers judge their authors by their ability to *write*. The approach should be a written one. You may have the patience to wait until you have completed the entire manuscript, and submit this with, ideally, a short letter, a one or two-page outline of the book so that the publisher or his reader can immediately see the scope before becoming embroiled in the manuscript itself; also always send return postage in case the work is rejected. But you may well prefer to have at least an expression of encouragement from a publisher before writing the whole book, and some publishers themselves like to comment at an earlier stage. So it may be sensible to send the letter and the outline or synopsis, possibly accompanied by a specimen chapter (not the introduction, which is usually untypical) to demonstrate your ability to put the plan into execution. If you have already published a book, or even a major contribution to a journal or magazine, of course tell the publisher and perhaps send a copy of that too.

But whatever you do, *write*. Do not at this stage call or telephone. Publishers must judge authors on their ability to communicate on paper, and even a short letter conveys some impression of that ability or lack of it. You will not, at least as yet, be judged for your ability to shine in a television interview. An important secondary reason for writing is that letters and synopses can be circulated among staff and outside advisers at the publisher's convenience. Meetings between publishers and authors are sometimes extremely fruitful, and often friendships develop, but let the publisher take the initiative. Even if you do not receive a reply to your first letter for some weeks and feel it necessary to chase him, do so in writing.

All this may seem obvious, but one of the biggest trials in the publisher's life is the number of people—including friends, and friends of friends, and the friends of friends of your most distant relations—who hope to gain some initial advantage by making personal contact. "You cannot trust the mails these days," is the commonest argument used for seeking an appointment. "I had better come with it myself." If you really cannot trust the mails, deliver the parcel to the publisher's door *anonymously*.

There are of course enterprising publishers and unenterprising, thorough and careless, and like anyone else they have good days and bad days. But a manuscript, or part of a manuscript, or just a synopsis, backed by a simple letter explaining the purpose of the book and the readership in mind, your qualifications, previous publications and other relevant facts, will in most firms on most occasions receive the consideration it deserves, and no amount of oral persuasion will make an iota of difference. But make sure you give the publisher all the facts: have you had a previous book published by another firm or do you have evidence of a growing public interest in your subject?

Build a Partnership

Although there are 35,000 new titles published in this country every year, it is nevertheless difficult for a new author to get published. No one has been able to determine the number of manuscripts which are sifted through and discarded in order to get down to the 35,000 figure, but the number obviously reaches astronomical proportions. However, let us immodestly suppose that this book has been sufficiently helpful to you in signing a contract with a publisher. Let us further suppose that in this instance you had not fully completed the book, but that the contract resulted from an outline and a specimen chapter; you agree to complete the book by a certain date. An increasing number of books are now arranged for in this way. The contract wiil undoubtedly contain a protective clause (especially if you are a new author), such as "subject to the publisher's acceptance of the completed manuscript," so that he does not commit himself to publishing your work should its quality be below that of the sample. (Contracts and financial matters are dealt with in the two following chapters.)

If you are working for a publisher along these lines, ideally you should seek to build up a partnership. Both partners should accept their responsibilities and seek to develop the potential in the other. Both sides should immediately notify the other if there is any basic change of plan—the author if he meets with an accident or is promoted and moves, if he finds a massive new source of information, or if anything else happens to disrupt his schedule, the publisher if he wants to change the proposed plans in any substantial way—as he may occasionally have good reason to do.

If a book has been commissioned for delivery a year or two hence, an occasional progress report (say once every six months) may be welcomed by the publisher or even sought by him, especially nearer to completion date. If the author is unhappy or in difficulties with a certain aspect of his book, the publisher should be pleased to receive warning in good time and to be given the opportunity to offer advice (and perhaps arrange a meeting with the author). If the author is preparing roughs for maps, it will be sensible for him to check that the publisher likes a sample. The unexpected appearance of a rival book on the same subject might be another occasion for an exchange of letters, to explore the possibility of changing the emphasis of the new book so as to lessen duplication. If the subject suddenly becomes topical, it may pay to see if completion and publication can be expedited.

All publishers and authors should welcome such communications with a purpose. The author however should realize that though he may find nothing more fascinating than writing letters about his book, the publisher will be more matter of fact, having seen books written before. Curiously, the authors who write the longest and most frequent letters are often those slowest to get down to the actual grind of completing the book itself. It is the book that the publisher is waiting for, not a pile of correspondence about the difficulties of writing it or promises about its ultimate quality. Keep necessary letters short and to the point. Long and complicated ones may not get properly read and digested, and essential information or requests may therefore be overlooked—especially if the letter is handwritten. These days virtually all business is done by typewritten letters, and a long, handwritten scrawl will almost certainly be the last item examined in the mass of paper arriving by that day's mail.

Conversely, some authors not merely lack the courtesy to tell their publisher when something goes wrong, but even ignore inquiries about what has happened to their overdue manuscript. If delays or difficulties arise and your publisher asks what has happened, the situation must be explained, warts and all; at least he should be able to offer constructive sympathy instead of sourly writing you off as a dead loss. A high credibility rating is one of an author's most valuable assets, and false promises and dour silences may be paid for dearly later.

If your completed manuscript is submitted past the outside date stipulated in your contract, the publisher has every legal right to withdraw from the agreement. Publishers are generally fair about this, however, and proper advance notices of delays with good and logical reasons are usually accepted by him. He would not have offered a contract in the first instance had he not wanted to publish the book. But he has schedules to meet and "face to save" with his colleagues and with the booksellers, if the book has been announced. In some instances, if so stated in the contract, he may even have the right to demand that you refund the cash advance if the delay in manuscript delivery persists.

Waiting for the Publisher's Reaction

Your manuscript is complete, and you duly send it to the publisher. What should you now expect from him? Some kind of immediate acknowledgment should reach you, but this is no clue to the publisher's reaction. The editor concerned may indeed be on a holiday, or working through a pile of waiting manuscripts, or feel that he needs to consult a colleague or outside expert before making any personal comment, even if the book has been commissioned.

Reading a book in manuscript form, and studying

illustrations, takes time and concentrated energy, and in smaller firms has to be fitted in by a few top people who also deal with much of the daily routine of publishing as a whole. Some degree of patience is required, and this is not the time to start writing letters, least of all to correct minor mistakes which may be discovered after the manuscript was mailed; a chance to put these right will occur later and loose slips of "additional copy" are merely a nuisance now.

Ultimately, of course, anyone may have justification to hint that he has been kept waiting for too long. But if your patience will stand it, keep quiet for two months. There is no excuse for publishers to procrastinate unnecessarily, and a delay of more than two months before giving at least a first reaction should score a bad point against the firm. But it does of course depend on the length and complexity of your work, and allowances have to be made for the inevitable hazards of Christmas, summer holidays, illnesses, postal delays and so on.

If your manuscript suddenly arrives back by mail without warning, read the accompanying letter before becoming despondent. It has not necessarily been rejected, since even if the publisher is basically enthusiastic he may ask you to change the emphasis here and there, to reduce the length to the agreed number of words if you have written far too much, to supplement a thin patch or to check certain facts. Once the manuscript is accepted, almost certainly you will get it back before the typesetter sees it; if it returns at this early stage, it will be because the publisher has some points he wishes you to reconsider before it goes to the copy-editor. As said earlier, publishers are not infallible, but their experience with books is greater than that of individual authors, especially new authors; they rapidly spot any section which let down the standard of the book as a whole, and the probability is that their requests for you to make certain changes will be justified—commercially, prestige-wise or both. Of course you will want to consider these requests seriously, especially if they involve a substantial amount of rewriting, but make sure of your ground before you dig in your toes and refuse to cooperate.

Sooner or later your book will be copy edited. Different firms mean differing things by the term copy editing, but it usually involves house styling where the author has not done it himself, smoothing of ugly sentences and corrections of grammatical errors. It may go further and include the rearrangement of certain passages into a more logical sequence, and even the complete revision of some pages, this being more likely if you are an amateur author and the publisher does not feel you have the capacity or professional touch to make these more drastic changes yourself. Questions of libel or offensive matter will be raised by the copy editor, who may also ask the author to check on certain facts and make other suggestions—whether or not the main editor has already asked for one set of changes.

If the copy editing is purely of a detailed nature and the author has already had the manuscript back to make any more radical changes, all should then be ready for typesetting. But if the copy editing involves substantial revision, the author should certainly be asked to make a final check through the manuscript; in effect this means asking him to agree to the changes, and now is the moment to raise any specific objections to what the copy editor has done. Again the author should consider changes and suggestions on their merit and not oppose them on principle; but if anything has been cut out that you urgently want left in, you should discover the fact and point it out, since the publisher will assume that you have accepted the manuscript as you return it to him and will not be pleased for you to "restore" a sentence on an already full page at proof stage. It helps if the author uses a colored ink for any final changes so that the copy editor can check that these weave in satisfactorily and make no departure from the consistent house style.

Timetables and Proofs

After copy editing, there will inevitably be a long gap before
101

the next stage: galley proofs. Just how long a gap depends on many factors—how quickly your publisher is used to working, whether a suitable copy editor is available, what other books in the same series or books potentially competing for the same market may be in the pipeline already, how busy the typesetters are. A happy standard timetable once the finished manuscript has been accepted and if necessary amended by the author might be:

January: Manuscript given to copy editor.

March: Copy editing completed and manuscript returned to author for final check.

April: Manuscript sent by publisher to typesetter (on a date arranged with the typesetter back in say February, meaning that the time table would immediately have gone wrong had the author not completed his final check within a reasonable period).

June: Proofs received by publisher and sent on to author.

July: Three or four weeks after proofs are received, they are returned to the publisher and returned by him to the typesetter, the index following a few days later and of course having to be proofed separately.

August: Corrections completed, camera-ready copy sent to printer. Printed flat sheets sent by the printer to the binder.

September: Bound copies available from the binder.

November: Publication, a minimum of four and more usually six weeks after the delivery of the bound copies.

It can be done more quickly, but that kind of schedule involves overtime for both the publisher and his printer, wear and tear, and dislocation of other projects only justified by extreme topicality. It may be sensible to elongate the schedule because the book concerned would be best published in a particular month; for a guide book the best publication month might be January or February and there would be no point in rushing for October publication even if the manuscript were edited in March. Publishers have to balance their lists, not bringing out too many books in total or too many in the same field, at one time. The example is anyway based on straightforward books

102

going without hitch at any stage straight into page proofs. If heavy editing, or the additional galley-proof stage has to be added, at least another two months will normally be needed.

An efficient publisher should tell his authors when they may expect proofs and what kind of proofs, and when they must be returned duly corrected if the publication schedule is to be kept. He should also give warning if the forecast date of arrival of proofs is not going to be met, because the typesetter is running late. For his part, an efficient author should keep time free for the proofing period, and do his best to meet the publisher's date for the return of the proofs. If he cannot meet it, he should say so at once. If you cannot make your own index, the publisher will probably be able to arrange for it to be done for you, but he must be given adequate time to do so since professional indexers plan their work well ahead and may not have the required dates free.

Production schedules, which tie down each operation not just to a specific month but to an actual day within that month, are not made for fun. They seek to secure an orderly progression of work and to make the best use of the publisher's, printer's and binder's resources. If proofs are returned late, even by ten days, publication on the chosen date may prove impossible. The printer who has kept one period free for handling your book may not be able to handle it ten days later, since another book will be scheduled to go on the machine then. Even if he can print your book just the ten days later so that the proposed publication date is kept, sales may suffer since advance copies will not be available so far ahead and the publisher's salesmen will find their task harder.

Normally an author will be allowed two to three weeks to read and correct each set of proofs, and be expected to supply an index within a week of returning the page proofs. That will often mean hard, concentrated work, and planning well ahead. For instance, if the author wants a colleague in a different part of the country to comment on the proofs, time could be saved by asking the publisher to send a copy direct.

As well as returning the proofs and the index on time, they

103

should be presented in a businesslike manner. It goes without saying that proof corrections should be kept to the minimum (see chapter 13), and this includes helping the publisher and typesetter by minimizing changes even where the printer himself has slipped, though obviously any real mistake or omission has to be rectified.

A publisher who keeps to his part of the bargain and who uses a typesetter whose general standard of work is high deserves such support as you can give him. But if you have waited a year or more for proofs, and they then arrive without notice, and contain many stupid errors, your annoyance will be understandable. Make allowances, however, for the fact that while you are probably only dealing with a single book, the publisher will have many on his schedule and must regulate the progress of the book. No doubt publishers do not always bother to explain what is happening and why, and that of course is regrettable; but they will have their own ways of doing things and you may have to abide by them arbitrarily. But do all in your power to make your publisher give adequate guidance and direction. If he does not volunteer proofing and publication dates, press him for them. Warn him if you are going on a vacation soon after the proofing period. A month before the proofs are due, check if they will be coming on time.

Publicity

One matter tends to cause a quite disproportionate amount of trouble. That is the question of when and how an author should tell his publisher about his views on the way his book should be publicized, sold and generally exploited.

The new author often itches to get started on the publicity campaign and bombards the publisher with suggestions even before the manuscript is finished. He may then be irritated, perhaps months later, to be asked for the information all over again by the publisher, who possibly expects it all to be set out on a formal questionnaire. The author may reply that he has given the information already; he may give part of it again, but in his rush or irritation forget the rest and subsequently ask the publisher to consult previous letters. It does take some application to sit down and pour out information about yourself, your contacts, the societies that might be interested in the book, and so on, all at one go. But it must also be obvious that it is impossible for the publisher to build up an adequate picture unless he has some system, and that while the publicity department may not want to know about a book to be published twelve months hence, when the time comes to consider the campaign the staff do genuinely need *all* the information at once. Many a sale has been lost, because some essential aspect of promotion has not been revealed or considered at the proper time or has been lost in letters chiefly concerned with other matters; at least occasionally this has resulted from authors being unwilling to go over ground they reckoned they had previously covered, even though the letters concerned may have been sent to quite different people in the publishing organization.

Many firms ask the author to write a draft blurb—the description, usually of 100-300 words, that goes on the front flap of the jacket and also appears (perhaps abbreviated) in the catalogue. The emphasis is on *draft* since the publisher himself will usually revise what the author sends in, using his own judgment and his assessment of the book market. But even if the author provides only the rough material, his help can be invaluable in summarizing just what his book has aimed to do. The blurb is, of course, intended to tell a potential purchaser in a bookshop just what the book is about; it should not be a paragraph about the author himself. There may however be room for some details about the author, possibly with a photograph, on the back flap. Most publishers welcome photographs of their authors to keep on file.

Authors are also usually invited to suggest which newspapers and magazines might usefully be given review copies; a skeleton list of periodicals may be sent for guidance. Considered suggestions will be treated seriously, but to tick off every paper on the skeleton list shows only enthusiasm, not discretion. Most newspapers will only publish reviews of books that have been sent to them officially, and publishers therefore usually ignore requests to send second copies to journalists at their home addresses, though if you happen to know a contributor to a particular paper there is no harm in mentioning the fact and the publisher may pass on an appropriate hint when sending the editor a copy. The publisher will probably decide for himself which popular daily and Sunday papers are worth a free copy, and will avoid wasting highly specialized books on newspapers that never review them. Though the publisher consults his own sources to insure thorough coverage, the author's personal knowledge of specialist and regional publications can be especially valuable in making certain that no vital gaps are left.

Publishers normally expect to send out something between 100 and 150 review copies of a non-fiction book costing $5.95 or more, covering radio and television services as well as the press. The more specialist the work, the smaller the number of periodicals likely to review it. Conversely, however popular the book's subject there must be some upper limit, since review copies cost money and, of course, will earn the author no royalty. Do not assume that your publisher is at fault if you hear that an editor has "not received" a copy; editors sometimes lend or even sell copies of books they do not intend to review, and then have to resort to the "not received" line if the author happens to ask directly if a review is going to be published. Publishers also receive many requests for review copies from newspapers and magazines not on their lists; some get their copies and useful publicity may result, but others are too clearly unsuitable papers whose editors or contributors are just begging a book for personal use. If a separate edition of your book is published in England, requests for review copies from the other side of the Atlantic will be passed on to the British publisher or distributor if these arrangements have been contracted for.

Review copies are of course sent out early to enable editors to get the reviews written and set up by publication date. They may go out even before the author has his own copies, and this is not unreasonable since the author does not immediately need copies for practical purposes and he can indeed upset booksellers by showing his book to people too soon.

In addition to review copies, it sometimes pays to send free copies personally to prominent people with influence in your subject field. But, again, free copies and the postage and handling cost the publisher money, and requests should not be made lightly. You can only reasonably expect the publisher to send to someone who might usefully aid sales, not to somebody to whom you have promised a copy because he gave you help. It is customary for you to fulfill that obligation yourself.

The publisher may also ask for your views on advertising and a brochure (though rarely). If so, bear in mind that it almost always pays to place at least small advertisements in specialist magazines and journals, and your personal knowledge of the most useful publications and positions within them will be welcomed. But an inch in the popular press may cost $150 and must earn $500 in sales to break even. Tell the publisher if you think good use could be made of a brochure or some form of information sheet describing your book and including an order form; there might be societies willing to circulate copies to their members, and you yourself might be able to use a hundred or so personally. But many brochures are printed without adequate thought being given to their use and end in the wastepaper basket. If the publisher produces other books on the same or related subjects, he may find it more economic and effective to produce subject lists. Do not object to back-list titles being advertised along with your new book: it shows that the publisher takes care to keep his older titles alive and your work will benefit from the same treatment in due course.

Subsidiary Rights

Certain kinds of books lend themselves to serialization or "onetime" condensation in newspapers and magazines, which may give useful publicity and boost ordinary sales as well as bring extra income—though long extracts of a specialized or regional book may give potential buyers too much of the content free of charge, and make them feel it is not worth buying the book itself. Most newspapers and magazines work well ahead, and early planning is needed.

The sale of special editions to Great Britain or of the British rights, and also the sale of the paperback rights are obvious ways of reaching more readers and bringing in more royalties. These financial aspects are considered in the next chapter. Translation rights are a different field; the author may know of some reason why his book could have an appeal in Scandinavia or Japan that might not occur to the publisher; it is fun to have your book printed in another language and may earn additional income. Book clubs open up another avenue, as there are general ones as well as specialists in certain subjects. There is also the possibility of film or television usage. Few non-fiction books lend themselves to full screen treatment, but occasionally a radio or television show will make use of material for a program inspired by a book or devised quite independently of it.

The author should pass all inquiries for such rights to the publisher, who will of course be entitled to keep a proportion of the receipts as laid down in the contract (see next chapter). Incidently, beware of the television producer or other seeker of your information and help who wishes to make use of your book but does not offer to get in touch with your publisher or offer you a fee direct. Some producers, no doubt working on tight budgets, hint that it will be in your interest to have your work publicized, but then make use of it without acknowledgment, perhaps because the context of the program simply did not allow any form of "plug" for the book.

After Publication

After publication, it will probably be the publicity department that you will be anxious to write to and to hear from. You may not think that your book has been adequately advertised, or you may have a last-minute idea for attracting more publicity.

You may want to discover what reviews have appeared so far, or send in a copy of a review in a specialist magazine that your publisher may not have seen. Some of this kind of contact can be useful and enjoyable to both sides, though enthusiasm can run too far. Authors who want weekly coverage of reviews could subscribe to a press-clipping service. Some publishers, incidentally, will send newspaper photostats of reviews. Good reviews should certainly be kept, in case they may prove useful in launching a new edition, though publishers vary widely in the importance they attach to reviews as a whole.

The author may also ask the publicity department about the book's sales, or write to the sales manager direct. He may point out that his book is missing from the shelves of an obvious specialist bookseller who should be stocking it; he may report complaints from his friends that the book cannot be bought anywhere in Decatur, Oklahoma. Again, a certain amount of such contact can be useful, and good sales managers and their representatives who service the bookshops should welcome genuine hints and even criticisms of their performance. But it is all too easy for the author to get his facts wrong. You may inquire about the number of copies that have been sold on publication date, if you like, but do not put in another request before the first royalty statement arrives which may be five months later. Make sure that any complaints are backed by fact. Authors can grumble that their books are unobtainable in certain bookshops simply because they did not immediately see them on display, sometimes even when in fact they were displayed, if looked for in the right place. Authors very often may not realize that the bookseller may have sold the copies he ordered and neglected to reorder. Moreover, many of the publisher's distribution problems originate with the problems of the bookstore. Most booksellers cannot cope with inventory control and what limited systems of control they use are generally inadequate to inform them of the exact moment that a book is out of stock. We mentioned earlier that there are 35,000 new titles published each year. Here are a few more relevant and

109

surprising statistics. There are about 3,500 bookstores. Only 500 of these are large enough to accomodate 50 percent or more of these new titles. The 3,000 small dealers must wait for favorable reviews in their geographic area or wait for consumer requests. In the case of a college bookstore, the manager must usually wait for the recommendation of a member of the faculty. In short, *distribution* is the main problem of publishing. Virtually anyone can get a book manufactured, but getting it exposed to the buying public is quite another matter. So before you take your publisher to task because a particular store did not have your book at a particular time, try to remember that your publisher is far more vexed over this situation than you are; he didn't have all those books printed just to languish in his warehouse. If you want to make sure, ask an assistant. But regularly to do the rounds of bookshops checking up on the display and sales of a book is distinctly not useful.

You will probably want to buy some copies yourself. The author usually receives six free copies and is allowed to buy more at trade terms (normally at a discount of 40 per cent) subject to the strict understanding that he does not resell copies at less than the full published price (see chapter 9). When ordering books for your own use, do so in a separate formal note and not in a letter dealing with other matters. (This point, like many in the book sounds almost stupidly obvious yet needs making.) Many authors tack an order to the end of a letter addressed personally to the managing director or editor, or even begin a letter on editorial or publicity matters with a request for copies that amounts to an order. Most publishers are departmentalized organizations, their order, invoicing and fulfillment departments often being in different buildings, perhaps in different towns, from the editorial offices, and letters containing mixed requests add unfairly to the burden of administration, and cannot be promptly processed.

If the book starts off selling well, you may figure that the publisher must be making a substantial amount of money, and that you could do with some for your new car or household repairs. Do you ask him for a check in advance? Rarely. Some contracts may stipulate advance payments of some kind, and the author may expect an additional interim payment. If some hundreds of dollars have been earned for you a month after publication and you would otherwise have to wait six months, then by all means ask and most firms will give the request sympathetic consideration. However, very few publishers will give advance royalties if they are not contractually obliged to do so. They want to recoup their production, promotion and overhead costs first. But the publisher is not obliged to pay before the stated day; also, even if the book has sold well it does not follow that the bookshops and wholesalers have yet settled their accounts. Also bear in mind that a large initial sale of your book may be what is known in the trade as an "advance sale," i.e. books purchased by booksellers but not as yet by consumers; these books may yet be returned to the publisher if unsold (see chapter 8). If you do get one lumpsum payment ahead of the date arranged, do not assume it will be a precedent for earlier payment. Each request has to be considered by a responsible person who will investigate the return of unsold copies which may occur at a future date. The publisher will try to avoid the possibility of the author overdrawing on future royalties.

Another Edition

Some of the books dealt with here should sell through successive editions if well handled by the right publisher. Your book may have become outdated, in which case you might be able to interest the publisher by pointing out that you have substantial new material and that the interest in the subject is rising. It is not unknown for the second edition to sell better than the first, especially when a gap of a year or so may occur.

Even if the first edition was printed by letterpress and the type has been destroyed, a reprint by photo-offset might be easy enough. In such cases any lines containing corrections are reset and pasted down over the lines they replace in a copy of the first

111

edition, or on reproduction pulls of the type that may have been thoughtfully taken for the purpose. It is therefore easy to change a date, or even to replace a ten-line paragraph by another of ten lines, but much more difficult to add or subtract lines. Any major changes in the subject will probably have to be covered in an additional chapter or in an entirely rewritten last chapter or epilogue. The point has already been made that topical allusions and forecasts can seem ridiculously out-of-date very quickly and that all such potentially ephemeral material is best concentrated in one place, preferably the last chapter or an epilogue, where it can be easily changed for any reprint.

Authors should of course record any mistakes found in the original edition and keep material for a possible reprint available. Even if the basic hardback edition has not sold well enough to make a reprint likely, there may be a paperback, bookclub, school or foreign-language edition which should be corrected and brought up-to-date.

To Be Remaindered

If, alas, the book has not sold well, the publisher may tell you he proposes to remainder it—to sell it off cheap. At this stage under the terms of the contract, most publishers offer the author copies at the reduced price and also the plates. Do not too meekly assume that the book has no future. If the publisher is selling it off because he makes a habit of doing so, or has changed his policy or the nature of his list, perhaps as the result of a merger with another firm, it may well be that a quite different publisher could be persuaded to accept the book. Even if no interested firm can immediately be found, once your publisher has definitely informed you that he is disposing of your book it may be wise to buy in as large a stock from him as you can (unless they are of a highly topical or ephemeral nature, sooner or later copies of some books may become scarce). Interest in the subject may revive, even if years pass before a second edition is possible.

112

Another Book?

Your first book has been launched. Now do you write another? And if so, who publishes it?

Many publishers like to see the reception accorded an author's first book and if happy may themselves suggest a sequel—especially if the author has proved businesslike. Certainly any suggestion you make will be sympathetically received. Conversely, if any suggestion for a second book is promptly turned down without the publisher hinting at an alternative idea, was it because previously he found you difficult to work with—your first manuscript failed to come up to expectation and had to be extensively copyedited or even partly rewritten at heavy cost, you were unhelpful over providing illustrations or proof correcting, or in some other way you stood out as an intransigent amateur? The publisher may be too polite to say so; he may think that even if he did tell you, and even if you did not take offense, you would still cause a disproportionate amount of trouble on future books.

But at least nine out of ten authors whose first books have done reasonably well would be welcomed in the list again if a good idea could be offered or found. Indeed, a close relationship with an author who produces a succession of books over the years is a most satisfying experience for a publisher. Continuity makes extremely good sense; you get to know the publisher, his staff and their ways, and you appreciate each other's problems and attitudes; they get to know you, and enjoy hearing about the progress of your children and your move to a new home or job. One of your books helps to sell another. The fact that you have produced a third or fourth title could be the crucial factor in persuading the publisher to reprint the first when it goes out of print. Bookshops find ordering easier if all an author's books come from the same firm.

Some young authors believe they should appear in as many different publishers' lists as possible in order to make a name for themselves. They are wrong. Of course, if you write a second book of a very different type, or if you receive a specific invitation to contribute a volume to an established series published by another firm, some break in continuity may be inevitable. But the really successful author normally has one main publisher, works closely with him, and only goes elsewhere when strictly necessary. He should confide in his main publisher, and expect to be kept in the picture about that publisher's other developments in the same field. He also expects his books to be given new editions whenever feasible. If such an association does not work smoothly, then you have chosen the wrong firm in the first place, or possibly you are the victim of changed policy following a takeover and should switch all your future titles to another publisher and start creating confidence afresh. To do this, however, you may require the publisher's permission, since most contracts oblige the author to give the publisher first refusal on the next book.

8

YOUR CONTRACT

YOUR CONTRACT

How Important?

People's reactions vary sharply when confronted with a legal document. Some authors are eager to sign their contract for a new book without taking even a cursory glance at it. Others virtually rewrite the entire thing. Some place implicit trust in their publisher; others display the maximum suspicion, assuming him to be guilty of trying to cheat until he proves himself innocent. Some think it unwise or too risky to question something they genuinely dislike; others feel they might look amateurish if they did not bargain and try at least a modicum of changes. Finally, some demonstrate their contempt for formalities by scrawling only their initials and then in the wrong place, missing the place over which they have been asked to sign.

On the whole too much rather than too little fuss is probably made about the kind of contract we have in mind here—an agreement between a publisher and an author over the arrangements for the publication of a single book. Of course the approach should not be sloppy, important points should be carefully checked, and signing should be done at the appropriate place. But normally only the one book is concerned,

117

which means that except in unusual cases the sum of money involved will be much less than in the sale of a house, for instance. Again except in unusual cases, many of the standard contingencies provided for in the contract will never apply—film rights in the case of a mathematical textbook, for example.

Most publishers have taken considerable care in the preparation of their standard contract, which is usually a printed form with spaces for the author's name, individual book's tentative title, contents and terms to be completed in typewriting. But it is hard to produce any form that pleases everyone, and an inordinate amount of time can be wasted by authors questioning the validity of certain clauses more or less standard among all publishers. Some authors even submit the contract to their attorney to read, and again great waste of time can result from the attorney querying something that is standard trade practice. The attorney, remember, will be paid for his work, while the publisher will have to fit it into his daily routine. (Publishers do not usually have special legal departments; garages don't either, and a new car is likely to cost more than at least the first edition of a non-fiction book will earn in royalties.) So take into account that while the contract may have novelty value for you, it has none for your publisher. He will have to make sure that any change from standard procedures is understood and carried into effect throughout his organization, which in itself can be expensive.

Most publishers feel that whenever authors and lawyers get to work on redrafting clauses, they not only choose different clauses to attack (if everyone condemned the same provision there would indeed be a case for amending the standard form), but have the supreme knack of missing the very points which could be most important in the long run.

A specimen contract for your guidance is included with explanatory notes; see chapter 12. Though most contracts have the same basic construction, obviously those of different firms reflect the character of their lists, fiction publishers being especially concerned with subsidiary rights, publishers in special areas with arrangements for illustrations, and so on.

Title and Contents

In most cases, a "working title" is agreed upon for contractual purposes. Publishers (and oftimes authors) prefer this to a final title because new ideas occur throughout the process of writing and editing a book.

Many contracts mention the length of the book, if it has not yet been fully written, and if the agreed length is say 70,000 words you should satisfy yourself that you can produce something between 65,000 and 75,000 words without undue padding or compression. In the case of an art book, some publishers also like to decide the number of plates at the contract stage. All this does not necessarily close the door to later discussion, but clearly if you have agreed to write the work in 70,000 words, and supply 16 pages of illustrations you cannot insist that the publisher accepts as it stands: your completed manuscript of 120,000 words plus photographs for 48 pages of illustrations. This example would in fact about double the publisher's costs, and the market might well not stand a book at twice the price even if it were twice as large.

Territory and Rights

The author is usually expected to grant the publisher the exclusive use of the book in a defined territory and for a defined period of time. These points deserve close attention.

The defined territory might be the United States and Canada or it might be the world. Generally, the average contract allows the American publisher full world rights. This means that the publisher's subsidiary rights division and his foreign literary agents will usually try to sell the work to publishers in other countries, splitting the net proceeds from these sales with the author on a 50-50 basis, less any costs incurred as a result of this sale.

In the case of the non-English speaking countries, the publisher will try to sell the translation rights, and the foreign publisher will produce the book from scratch. In the case of a British sale, this very often means the British Commonwealth (excepting Canada), Australia, New Zealand, India, etc.

In the case of Britain, a publisher may use the American plates, which represent a major factor in the cost of producing the book by eliminating typesetting costs. Rarely, however, will the British publisher contract for bound books from the United States because their costs for printing and binding are less than ours. By contracting in advance with a British publisher for sale of an American book in the form of plates, films, or sheets, the American publisher decreases his gamble enormously in the first instance, and the author gets an additional income.

Because of the disparity in production costs between America and Britain, an American publisher will sometimes elect, after selling the British rights, to produce the book in England; this, in effect gives him a dual savings: a larger run and cheaper production costs.

In the case of books without many illustrations and of wide British interest, an author or his agent may sometimes elect to retain the British and foreign-language rights. He remains free to approach overseas publishers directly, thereby possibly receiving royalties on other publishers' editions. However, it should be pointed out that selling overseas rights demands substantial know-how which few individual authors are likely to possess, while the publisher undoubtedly has contacts with many foreign literary agents.

Many contracts devote much space to the question of subsidiary rights. With fiction and other literary types of work, the sales of subsidiary rights may prove extremely rewarding; some novels are published solely for the rights income they are likely to generate. But subsidiary rights are usually less important with definitive non-fiction, and the contracts of publishers specializing in such works or educational books may cover the whole subject in a single sentence. The author should check that he will receive at least one-half of any income from the translation of the work into a foreign language, and
120

serialization or extract published in a newspaper or magazine.

Paperback rights are obviously more important. They are almost invariably controlled by the publisher of the hardback who expects to split the income 50-50 between himself and the author. That there is a demand for the book in paperback form may be due to his original success in promoting the hardback edition, whose sales may suffer once the cheaper version is on the market. But authors of definitive non-fiction should remember that it is almost always the hardback that accounts for most of the income. Occasionally a few publishers may let the original hardback edition go out of print still expecting to enjoy the paperback income while unwilling to relinquish the hardback rights. The author then receives no hardback royalties and only half of the less rewarding paperback ones.

Term of Contract

In these days of takeovers and changes of policy, perhaps the most vital clauses in contracts are those relating to what happens when the original hardback edition goes out of print. Ideally authors should seek the return of *all* rights to themselves if the hardback edition goes out of print and the publisher declines to reprint it within a reasonable period. But the appropriate clause now more usually reads "If the work shall become out of print and not be available in any edition issued by the Publisher or authorized by him," while some publishers in fact expect to reserve the right to sell all rights in perpetuity (including even the hardback rights to another hardback publisher in due course) of any book they have once had in their list.

Once more, the best protection the author can give himself is to choose a publisher who will not let a worthwhile book still in demand go out of print indefinitely, or who if he does not feel able to reprint will have the grace to release all rights, or at least the income from them in a reasonable amount of time. See how the contract for your book is worded in this important respect. Do not, however, be too harsh on the publisher regarding the length of period he may request before the rights revert to you, if no reprint is produced, for there are a variety of reasons why it may pay to delay a reprint. Some agents seek to have rights revert to the author if the work remains out of print for only six months; two years seems a more reasonable time, since a judicious gap between editions may be beneficial or the publisher may want to delay slightly to prevent clashing with other titles in the same series or on the same subject.

Another essential point to check is the period that must elapse before the publisher can produce a cheap edition, or remainder or otherwise dispose of the stock. Two years is not an unreasonable minimum before any consideration should be given to reducing the price of the hardback edition, even though the author will probably be wise to agree to the production of an additional bookclub or other special edition at a lower price. Experience shows that very rarely indeed do bookclub or other *special* editions hurt the sale of the main hardback edition, and if they produce relatively little revenue (royalties again normally being calculated on a net-receipts basis), at least it is extra; but any drop in the price of the main hardback edition, even temporarily as for a book sale, may irrevocably damage future prospects. As said in the last chapter, most contracts enable the authors to buy copies of the book and plates should the publisher feel that the demand has ceased and want to remainder or even destroy the remaining stock. This protection can be extremely useful where the publisher has lost interest as the result of change of ownership or policy.

But first there should be at least a modest period of sales. Having discussed the extent of the publisher's rights, both geographically and in time, the remaining contract points can perhaps be best discussed under the headings of the author's and the publisher's responsibilities.

The Author's Responsibilities

The author will be expected to confirm that the work is his
122

own property, that if any copyright permissions are needed he will provide the publisher with the necessary written releases, that there is nothing of a libelous or scandalous nature in his manuscript, and normally that he will indemnify the publisher against any actions or costs should the work be imperfect in any of these respects.

An American copyright lasts for 28 years and is renewable for another 28 years; there is now a bill before Congress to change the law to conform to the British copyright law which allows the rights to exist on any work for fifty years after the death of the author or artist.

Normally a very short extract of copyright material may be used to demonstrate a point without the need to obtain copyright permission. For more substantial extracts permission must be obtained from the copyright holder, especially if they are quoted for their own sake rather than as a (properly acknowledged) reinforcement of your argument. Most publishers expect authors to provide photographs at their own expense, again with any copyright complications cleared. A statement does not necessarily have to be untrue to be libelous; a man's reputation and business may be damaged by the circulation of a perfectly true statement. Only in very special cases is it worth running the risk of libel proceedings; if in any doubt leave out the passage concerned. Where there is some overriding reason for the inclusion of a statement you feel could possibly constitute libel, then explain it when you send the manuscript to the publisher.

Other responsibilities the author usually carries are to read and return proofs within a stated period (often three weeks), to make the index, and to undertake revisions to the book from time to time should new editions be required. The contract will normally be worded so that the publisher can deduct from the royalties the cost of having these operations done should the author fail to do the work himself. Indeed, most contracts go so far as to say that if the author does not complete the book itself by the due date the publisher may get it completed and deduct the cost from royalties or other monies due to the author. Such intervention is of course extremely rare, and though authors should try to honor their delivery dates, most publishers are long-suffering. Eventually, if the author fails to deliver the manuscript, and more particularly if he refuses to say what progress he has made and when he hopes to complete it, the publisher may give notice that he intends to cancel the contract. But this happens only in extreme cases. When the author of an existing book that needs revising is dead or infirm, or positively wishes someone else to do the work, the publisher may engage a suitable substitute and deduct the cost from royalties.

Another penalty to watch for is the area of author's alterations (AA's). After submitting the final draft of your manuscript and the book is initially set into type, all subsequent changes are very costly for the publisher. Invariably, there will be a contractual clause penalizing you financially for an excessive number of changes, additions or deletions from this time forward. "Excessive" will be defined by the publisher in the contract.

Finally, the author may be asked to give the publisher an option on his next one or two books. The option clause usually states something like: "The Publisher shall have the first option of reading and the first option of publishing the Author's next work on terms to be agreed with the Author." Since the author can anyway reject any terms offered him, the clause really does no more than say that the author should keep his publisher informed about his next book or books. New authors should have no hesitation in accepting this. Even established authors who ask for the clause to be deleted because they have already committed work elsewhere should keep their publishers informed about their plans. If an author writes a number of different types of book, he sometimes asks for the words "of the same kind" or "on the same subject" to be inserted, qualifying the option so that he is free to take other works elsewhere.

The Publisher's Responsibilities

The publisher normally guarantees to produce the book

within a certain time after the delivery of the complete manuscript and illustrations, but the author's degree of protection is usually whittled away by the addition of such words as "unless prevented from doing so by circumstances beyond their control." The circumstances beyond the control of certain publishers may of course be bad planning. Many books that should have been published within twelve or eighteen months of the delivery of the manuscript do not appear for thirty-six or even forty-eight months, for no better reason than that nobody has come round to attending to them. Yet again, try and choose an efficient publisher. If you are unlucky, remember this clause and press the publisher to say what particular circumstances have been beyond his control; but press early, since if you hear nothing at all for two years it could just be that nothing has happened and that all still has to be done.

Most agreements spell out the fact that the whole of the physical production of the book shall be controlled by the publisher, and that he can determine the price charged for it, how many free copies are used to promote its sale, and so on. In return, of course, the publisher normally accepts the whole of the risk of the venture, the author's financial liabilities being limited to excess author's alterations; he is normally charged for any changes he makes in excess of 10 per cent of the original cost of composition. Since corrections are infinitely more expensive than original composition, this "free" allowance of 10 per cent does not in fact buy very much. Correction of printer's errors are not charged to author or publisher, and should be made in a different color ink, using standard correction marks.

The contract of course states what remuneration the publisher is to make to the author. Finance (including rates of royalties) is dealt with within the next chapter. The only point that needs mentioning here is the date on which royalties become payable. In the past they were almost universally paid half-yearly; today some firms reduce their bookkeeping by making an annual report and payment. On the whole this change is fair; it is in everyone's interest that overhead is kept to a sensible minimum. In an effort to keep down costs, many firms do not now make payments if the amount due is less than a

125

certain minimum, usually $100 during a six month royalty period.

The publisher states he will give the author so many free copies (usually six) and offers further copies at his usual trade terms, and perhaps even offers any book in his list at these terms. The clause about free copies causes publishers a quite disproportionate amount of correspondence, since many authors write to ask if the six can be increased to seven, eight, nine, twelve, twenty or a hundred. Ingenious are the reasons given to back these claims; most are rejected. Publishers exist to *sell* books! Should you wish to *purchase* additional copies, your contract usually states that you may do so at a 40% discount.

Joint Contracts

Before you become a "joint author" make sure it would not be as easy to do the whole job yourself, or at least to take the prime responsibility, the contract with the publisher being in your name, even if you do sub-contract certain parts to someone else and acknowledge that help on the title page or elsewhere.

In fact it is not unduly difficult to arrange a contract jointly in two people's names, each of them to be paid half the royalties. Problems begin to get serious when three or more are involved. Not only is there the matter of dividing royalties (perhaps small amounts years after the book has been published) into fractions, recording all the authors' changes of addresses, and so on, but the more people involved, the more they change their minds, and the more the likelihood of life's natural hazards hitting one of them. Seldom does a work planned with half a dozen joint authors come smoothly to fruition, all delivering their parts by the agreed date.

Put bluntly, a book by a number of different authors is less likely to get published than a comparable work by one or perhaps two. If there has to be more than a single author, the most efficient plan is for one alone to act as editor, or at least as spokesman, for the contract to be made with him, and for him to make private arrangements with the others—all that the others need is a formal exchange of letters with the leader to protect their position. Failing any agreement of that kind, the publisher may have no alternative but to purchase the work of the individual contributors outright, though perhaps still paying a small royalty to the chief author or editor. The problem in selling work outright is that the incentive interest for the contributor is removed and neither the publisher nor you can know what sum should be paid.

Later Use

You may seldom have the occasion to glance at your contract once your book has been published, or once it has gone out of print and seems to be dead. But you or your descendants could possibly want it many years later.

As said earlier, an American copyright at the present time expires maximally 56 years after publication (if renewed), and many authors publish their best books when they are still relatively young. Books which enjoyed only a modest success when they appeared in the 1910s, 1920s and 1930s are being reprinted today, the authors' descendants drawing the royalties—though in some cases the reprinting publishers find it hard to trace those descendants (especially if the original publishers have ceased business) and the original contracts never come to light. The loss of the contract should not in itself prevent republication, of course, but if available it might clarify an issue otherwise uncertain. Its existence might act as a reminder that you once published a certain book or books and so encourage your children or grandchildren to take steps to keep your name and ideas alive and receive some belated income for themselves.

The best place to keep your contract is with your will, which itself should mention your copyrights. Make your instructions as specific as possible. Even if any royalties are to be divided equally between a number of beneficiaries, can you nominate one to have power to act on behalf of all in dealings with publishers? Joint executors scattered round the world and perhaps with no knowledge of publishing practice are even more unpopular with publishers than living joint authors.

9

AUTHORSHIP AND FINANCE

AUTHORSHIP AND FINANCE

Not Purely for Money

Books should not be written *solely* for money. If your objective is to make large sums quickly, there are easier ways of doing it than through authorship. Conversely, if you specifically want to write a book, whether because you have something to communicate or because you wish to build up your reputation in some field, you will have views on how it should be done and will take more than minimal care over it; you will not be making money the sole criterion of the project's value.

Publishers learn to beware of the author who says he has no other interest in book-writing than earning money—and of the would-be author who starts by placing undue emphasis on requesting the financial aspects. Books from such people are usually superficial. They do not sell well. They may be bad bargains for publishers and they do not enhance their writers' prestige.

The public is far more discriminating than most newcomers to authorship and publishing perhaps believe. Good books genuinely do a lot better than bad ones. But it takes time to sort out the wheat from the chaff. The quality of the work may not make much difference to the size of initial orders or indeed perhaps to the sales during the whole of the first year. Thereafter the gap widens, the potboiler dying a natural death while the quality work settles down to a steady sale year by year, perhaps with occasional fillips as new and revised editions appear.

Full or Part-Time Authorship?

The problem is that at the end of the first year after publication, which probably means two years since he completed the writing, and perhaps three years since he incurred the cost of much of the research, the thorough and competent writer may have received no greater royalties than if he had skimped the job. At this stage, therefore, his rate of payment per hour of work spent on the book will be positively less than had he rushed it. And if he is in a precarious financial position, such as having just married and bought a house, it may be no vast comfort to know that he may still be drawing royalties from the sale of his book when his first child gets married.

But there is no disputing the fact that responsible authorship of non-fiction books of the kind discussed here demands taking the long-term view. This means that the young man desperate for immediate spending money should not be writing a book at all, but selling his time some other way. His book may anyway be better if he can delay starting it till he is under less pressure. It also means that it is hard for anyone, however talented, to turn authorship successfully into a full-time profession.

The part-time author whose basic salary is provided by another job can afford to invest in his book, perhaps receiving the fruits of his labor spread over five, ten or even fifty years. If he writes a succession of books in his spare time, eventually he may receive substantial yearly royalties to supplement his basic income, and he may be in the happy position of knowing that these royalties may continue after he retires from his basic job, and that it would not matter unduly even if he lost that job or

131

retired early.

But except for a very small handful of famous people, full-time authorship is apt to be a grinding struggle to make ends meet. The man who lives by his writings has somehow to keep himself and his family—who are not likely to be content with a low standard of living—and is obsessed with his short-term financial problems. He cannot write what he would most like to write since that will not produce enough spending money. He is liable to be so taken up with today's financial problems that he cannot invest in the scholarly work that might assure him of a steady income five years ahead. In five years' time he will still be battling to make immediate ends meet. But by then his publisher (or publishers, for he usually has to be prolific enough to need several) may realize that he is producing a succession of potboilers.

There are nominally full-time authors who do not have to worry unduly about immediate money matters since they enjoy a private income or their wives or husbands earn the bread and butter. But except for the top 1 per cent (who will not be reading this book anyway) and those with other income, full-time authorship is not an expedient. So often one has seen the man who sought freedom in a freelance life become slave to the routine of writing what he does not want to write in order to keep the wolf from the door. Not only do his books tend to become potboilers, mere rehashes of his own and other people's previous works, but he is forever snatching at opportunities in journalism, broadcasting and lecturing to supplement his income, and may actually end up with less time (and less creative energy) for writing books than he would have if he gave five working days a week to some other job.

The best advice to the would-be author is to remain with a congenial job in some walk of life that will not use precisely those parts of his being that authorship demands. The journalist is potentially the worst of authors for the fairly solid type of book; however practiced his ability to communicate and marshal his thoughts, he cannot turn to writing his book with a fresh mind: the work is merely an extension of his daily job. The
132

university lecturer or the school teacher, the accountant, civil servant, technician, industrial consultant or lawyer, even the manual worker, bring greater spontaneity; and in any case their daily work and contacts develop their experience and feed them with material and ideas for their writing. This alone gives them the advantage over the full-time author whose reservoir of thoughts and material—and capacity for sitting endlessly at his desk—is apt to run dry.

So if your first one or two books should be outstanding successes, do not fall into the common trap of assuming you can maintain that success for the rest of your working life. By all means plan to retire a few years earlier to devote more time to writing, or deliberately let promotion bypass you in your main job so as to retain adequate free time; but avoid the all-too-real possibility of having to churn out two or three potboilers year by year because you have no other source of income and each successive book you publish sells less well than its predecessor.

But of course take your book-writing seriously. Be professional in all respects except in depending on it exclusively for your livelihood. Be professional even in striking the most sensible bargain with your publisher.

Methods of Remuneration

Basically there are three kinds of arrangements between authors and publishers:
(1) The publisher takes the risk involved in publishing and pays the author a royalty based on sales.
(2) The publisher takes the risk but buys the author's copyright outright for a lump sum.
(3) The author and publisher share the risk, or the author bears the whole of it, with some kind of subsidy or profit-sharing arrangement.

Most adult non-fiction books are covered by the royalty arrangement based on sales and selling price, which has much to commend it. Since both author and publisher have an interest in

133

the continuing success of a book, they are encouraged to work closely together. The author's reward is linked not only to the book's sales but to the price at which it is published; that price may steadily increase over the years, as costs of production rise, giving him some protection against inflation.

If the author sells the copyright outright to the publisher, the purchase price is likely to be far less than royalties would eventually earn. The lure of $1,000-$2,000 in outright payment when you need a new car or a world trip to gather material for the next book may be appreciable, but try to withstand it. Retain your equity stake in your creation. Remember that the interest in your subject may suddenly increase or there may be overseas or subsidiary rights possibilities that had not occurred to you; remember that if the book is reprinted the price of the second edition may be higher than that of the first. But the overriding objection to outright payments is perhaps that they are seldom equitable to both parties; either the publisher or the author is apt to feel he has had the bad end of the bargain—a feeling which does not help promote understanding if further books are to be produced. There are, of course, exceptions. Publishers of short books for children sometimes buy the texts outright on the grounds that the work involved for the writer was little more than jobbing journalism. The publisher of a symposium with ten contributors may want to pay a lump sum to each merely to ease the burden of administration—though even then the contributors might seek to retain certain rights, including perhaps freedom to use their own part in books of their own authorship at a later date.

The third kind of arrangement, involving the author in contributing to the costs of production ("vanity publishing"), needs approaching with care. Competition for publishable books is intense, and if your book has any commercial potential, it should be possible to find a publisher to nurture it—maybe with payment of only nominal royalties, and maybe with fewer illustrations than you might have preferred, but still risking the sinking of several thousand dollars of his own money into the venture without asking you to contribute. If all likely firms

134

(including perhaps a university press prepared to subsidize a few high-quality manuscripts of strictly limited appeal) turn you down on an ordinary royalty basis, the book should probably not be published at all, and if you do find a firm willing to produce it wholly or partly at your expense, you stand an excellent chance of losing your cash and of seeing that the other publishers were right in their decision not to risk theirs.

But, as to all rules, there are honorable exceptions. Printing is a mass-production process, and even a specialist publisher normally needs to be able to see a sale well into four figures before he can take the book into his list. There are some highly specialist books whose sales may never reach 1,000, or even 500, but which might nonetheless be welcomed by a small band of professional or other people. If the author has money to spare to support publication, there is no reason why he should not do so.

The author unable to get his work published in the ordinary way by a commerical publisher should be careful to avoid firms dealing mainly in "vanity" books. Give your subsidy to a reputable firm, conversant with the type of book concerned, the book will at least be properly and suitably produced, published and circulated as any ordinary book in which publisher as well as author has faith. But this will not necessarily be achieved by some of those firms that specifically exist to "publish" books at their authors' expense, often advertising their services in the newspapers. "Publishing" in such cases often means little more than printing. True, the books are announced as being available for sale to the trade, but the trade knows that the author will have had to pay for the privilege of "publication," which normally implies that no reputable publisher would accept the work at his own risk, or even with a subsidy, and that therefore the sales potential is negligible.

Vanity Publishing

A vanity press is really nothing more than a printer who is

willing, on a contractual basis, to print an author's manuscript. He "comes on" as a publisher but he is not a publisher in the true sense of the word. The primary way of recognizing a vanity publisher is by the contract he offers. Rather than receiving a small sum of money as an advance against royalties, the author is, instead required to pay a large sum of money for the full production of the book (editing, paper, printing and binding) as well as for the advertising and publicity. The author pays the publisher, the publisher does not pay him. With a legitimate publisher, the reverse is true.

There is nothing illegal about a vanity press. The author is over 21 and has signed a valid contract, albeit a one-sided one. Generally, the author who signs a vanity contract winds up with his basement full of books. In a regular publishing venture, the books belong to the publisher; promotion, distribution and sales are his obligation. In contrast, with almost every vanity contract, unsold books may wind up burned, shredded or otherwise destroyed, usually at the author's expense. Or, the author has to pay to bring them to his own premises.

Distribution attempts by a vanity press are minimal. The books generally sit in the warehouse—and once again the author pays, this time for storage.

The primary reason for lack of distribution is that bookstores generally will not carry vanity books. The bookseller knows that they are vanity jobs. The book reviewer is also aware of this and will not review them. The bookseller feels that if all the regular trade publishers have rejected a book, it could not be very saleable. In most cases, the book has indeed been rejected a number of times, but the author still feels that his work is worthy of publication. Because of this belief, he will pay to have it printed himself.

The primary means of identifying a vanity press is by its blatant advertising. Reputable publishers do not buy newspaper space to unequivocally solicit new manuscripts as vanity presses do. As a matter of fact, regular line publishing houses are besieged by many unsolicited manuscripts. They also have specific writers whom they commission for certain projects.

There is no way of identifying vanity presses as a group. In one sense, there are as many potential vanity presses as there are printers. There are several well known in the trade producing between 300 to 400 books per year.

There is no way of estimating how many people pay to have their own books published by vanity presses but it is safe to estimate that 90 per cent of these ventures are commerical flops.

Royalty Arrangements

The standard royalty rate for a hardbound book is 10 per cent of the full retail (list) price of the book. Generally, the contract calls for an upward sliding scale. Usually, this scale will be as follows:

> 10% on the first 5,000 copies
> 12-1/2% on the next 5,000 sold
> 15% all copies over 10,000 sold

However, there is nothing immutable about this scale. Elaborate specialty books with high production costs, text and technical books, inexpensive editions of juvenile books, as well as original paperbacks may start from a 5 per cent to 8 per cent royalty base.

The range of cash advances against royalties, however, is much wider. Many very small publishers do not pay any advance for the simple reason that they cannot afford them. These may be very worthwhile houses and are not necessarily to be eschewed because of this practice. Other small to medium-sized publishers usually maximize their advances at $5,000; most pay $1,000 to $3,000. Advances are usually paid as follows:

> 1/2 on execution of contract
> 1/2 on delivery of the completed acceptable manuscript
>
>   or
>
> 1/3 on execution of contract

137

1/3 on delivery of the completed acceptable manuscript
1/3 on publication

A lower rate of royalty is normally paid on export sales, and as has been mentioned, where the publisher sells copies at less than half the published price he usually pays a royalty on the basis of his "cash received" rather than the full published price. If the royalty rate is on a sliding scale, the point at which the higher percentage begins is normally calculated only on the ordinary domestic sales, export and special-edition sales at cheaper prices not being included. In other words if the royalty rate goes up to 12-1/2 per cent after the sale of 5,000 copies, the sale of a special edition to a foreign country of 2,000 copies will not be included in the 5,000.

As already stated, royalty rates are normally lower on paperbacks, and lower rates are also common with children's books and school textbooks designed to be sold in large numbers at low prices.

What about advances against the royalties the book is expected to earn? The author writing his first book may be offered a smaller advance, but established authors expect a larger one. Advances may be paid on signing the contract, on delivery or acceptance of the completed manuscript, or on publication, or divided between two or three stages. Normally only the famous professional author, or someone writing a book with enormous sales expectations, is paid an advance of any size on signing of the contract; with non-fiction books of the kind considered here the more normal arrangement might be an advance of $500-$1,000 on signing of the contract, of a set amount on delivery of the manuscript and an equivalent amount on publication of the book.

Publishers paying the largest advances are often those backed by big holding companies and with access to reserves of ready cash; but these include firms that sometimes suffer from poor management and lack of individual concern for their books, therefore operating a fairly ruthless policy of not reprinting moderately successful books and of remaindering
138

those that fall short of the sales target. Conversely, some of the best-run firms work on limited liquid-cash resources, and especially if they exploit long-term possibilities cannot afford to tie up too much money too far ahead of publication.

One final point: sometimes authors complain that their receipts are so small that publishers cannot notice paying them. This is not true. From the publisher's point of view it is perhaps unfortunate that royalties are calculated as a percentage of the full published price rather than as a proportion of their actual receipts. Thus while the author may receive only 10 per cent of the total money paid by the public on the purchase of his book, the publisher has to pay out a great deal more than 10 per cent of his receipts. Royalties are distinctly not a marginal consideration in publishers' balance sheets.

Taxation

While internal revenue agents make sure that taxpayers declare all taxable income, they do not always check that every allowance or expense has been claimed. It is unfortunately just not enough to leave everything to the Internal Revenue Service.

A case in point: an author filed his annual tax return, deducting the expenses incurred in order to earn an income as a freelance author and journalist. He was comfortably assured he was being treated fairly, and was saving the cost of professional accountancy advice. It was only years later, when he had other business and needed an accountant to deal with his more complicated tax affairs, that he realized he had been paying an unnecessary amount of tax. For a start the accountant, who then took over the whole of his personal finances, succeeded in making the internal revenue agent agree to something he had unsuccessfully pressed on a number of occasions. He had merely put forward a commonsense argument; the accountant quoted the exact wording of the relevant section of the Internal Revenue Code to prove that what he was seeking was in accordance with the law.

The emphasis is always on the law. Basic fairness and unfairness, and any consideration of ethics, do not really come into it. If the law is downright unfair and even unethical, you have to obey it. You also exploit its weak points. You cannot afford to pay up when the law is unfair to you, and also pay up when you feel it would be unethical to take advantage of a legal loophole or you cannot be bothered to make a claim that would involve some work. At any rate, if you do take the "heads you win, tails I lose" attitude, do not blame your publisher for not paying you enough to make your writings worthwhile.

Since most authors do not have the time or inclination to follow closely the changes in taxation law and practice, and since the law becomes ever more complicated, almost certainly it will be worthwhile employing a professional accountant—ideally a partner in a smallish firm or branch office of a larger organization who can give individual attention to the often quite complex tangle surrounding the financial transactions of publishing even a few books.

You might not feel it necessary to go to an accountant until the business of authorship really starts—say after the receipt of the first royalties. But whatever you do, make sure that you record all relevant expenditures from the very start of your project—while you are doing research, perhaps years before you actually put pen to paper. At worst these accumulated expenses will be offset against the income when it arises; at best they should be offset against your other income even before you receive your first payment from your publisher, and a reduction in your current tax liabilities may give authorship greater point in the eyes of both yourself and your wife (or husband). The IRS agent will of course need convincing that you are genuinely set to become an author before he starts allowing expenses to be offset against your other income—merely dabbling with the possibility of writing will not suffice.

Two especially important points about taxation should be understood by authors not wanting to pay more tax than necessary. The first concerns the schedule under which the profits of authorship are taxed; the second the accounting period, or tax year.

In any event, whether you are a full or a part-time author you would do well to consult an accountant.

What Expenses Qualify?

Broadly you can claim any expenditure that has been wholly and exclusively incurred in the pursuit of writing. But there is one very important qualification by the IRS. To make these deductions, you must be a *professional* writer. A professional writer is one who either can produce a *contract* from a trade publisher, or show *sales* of his own vanity book. In other words, you cannot claim deductions for unpublished works. You may classify yourself as professional even if you write part-time. The expenses need not be limited to any set proportion of the income, or indeed have any relationship to the eventual income expected, there being no law to tell you that you must make a profit out of your writing or other vocation. If you like to produce a painstaking piece of research at a high cost for a very limited market and your expenses vastly outstrip the income, that is your affair, though it would be only natural for the IRS agent to scrutinize such accounts more closely than those of a more profitable author and to question any marginal-sounding items such as heavy travel and hotel bills.

It will, incidentally, be obvious that authors who write about places and things generally have stronger evidence of the need to run up an expense account than the novelist, playwright or poet who depends mainly on his imagination. It pays to keep a detailed record so that you do not forget items when you come to make up the account at the end of the year and can substantiate claims if there are arguments. Noting the expenditure in a diary and analyzing it at the end is as convenient a method as any.

Office costs If you work at home on your book, even just occasionally, some household costs should be claimed: at least you will have used extra lighting and heating. Ideally you should

141

have a separate work den and charge the appropriate proportion of all household expenses, including repairs and decoration, cleaning, heating and so on. Thus if your study occupies one-eighth of the total area of the house, you charge one-eighth of the cost of external painting or of the fuel to run the central-heating system.

The total cost of telephone calls (and of the telephone rental if business calls predominate), postage, stationery, files and photographic films related to writing should of course be claimed.

Maintenance of library The cost of reference and related books which you maintain in order to pursue your career as a writer may be depreciated over a reasonable period of time, usually ten years. The cost of additions to the library may be added to the initial cost each year. Be sure to keep the receipts for all acquisitions. The cost of relevant trade and technical journals as well as newspapers is also a deductible expense.

Depreciation allowances These will almost certainly be given on capital items such as furniture or typewriters in your office. You may depreciate capital items such as typewriters, office furniture, tape recorders, etc. Here again, be certain to keep all receipts and invoices. Carpeting, bookshelves are also allowable. If a room in the home is used as an office, a reasonable portion of the cost of the rent and its attendant expenses may be depreciated. Also eligible for deduction are the actual costs incurred in obtaining a copyright (although the publisher generally attends to this for you). A professional accountant is especially useful in making certain that you have covered all expenses regarding your allowable deductions. His fee can be deducted also.

Subscriptions Subscriptions to organizations and societies connected with or useful for your writing work are deductible but the cost of attending the meetings and conferences of professional organizations does not always qualify. Press-
142

clipping agency subscriptions qualify.

Secretarial help If you employ an outside typist or secretary solely for work on your book, the expense should be charged in full.

Wife's or other relation's help Authors are often helped by relations, most frequently male authors by their wives who may sometimes genuinely give up other possibilities of earning for this purpose. Work should be paid for even when done within the family, and substantial and genuine savings in tax can often be achieved.

The wife must of course provide the services she is paid for, and the payments must actually be made, however the money is used thereafter. The wife may be paid for undertaking research in a library, for taking telephone calls and messages and making inquiries on the author's behalf, for reading and criticizing the manuscript and retyping it, and even for the office proportion of cleaning the home if there is a separate office. What she is paid must be reasonable in relation to the services she performs, of course, but again it must be emphasized that an author is not compelled to make a profit from his writing, and providing his wife's services are essential, they can be charged at the full current rates of pay for people doing such work even if the book will show a loss.

The wife is often deprived of her husband's company while he is writing a book, or the husband may feel neglected if the wife is the author, and joint participation in the project in some way or other may have constructive psychological as well as financial implications. It can be particularly fruitful if the non-author develops know-how that the author himself may lack: becoming, for instance, the photographer of the pair.

Payments to wives are most conveniently made on a fee basis for actual work performed. But regular and substantial payments may make it inevitable that she is classified as a regular employee of her husband, in which case income and

143

Social Security taxes must be deducted and reported quarterly on IRS Form 941.

Insurance and pension   You insure your library and claim the cost of the policy. If you are dependent upon writing for your livelihood it is worth considering a policy guaranteeing you a certain minimum income in the event of disability.

Accountant's fees   As stressed earlier, if your affairs become in the least complicated, engage a professional accountant; his fee is an allowable expense against income.

A Few Other Tax Points

Though it is generally only the writer of a best-seller who suffers from a sudden abundance of income, paying much more tax than were the income more evenly spread over a longer period, all authors should be aware that "averaging" provisions do exist, and should file IRS Schedule G if they elect to average income. Averaging, in effect, taxes high income of one year as if it were spread over a five-year period.

Since the earnings of most authors, from their regular jobs as well as from spare-time writing, will probably be rising year by year, the potential advantage of being able to transfer income backwards is obvious; but many factors, such as other income, changing personal allowances and the possibility of a drop or rise in the standard rate of tax, have to be borne in mind.

Incidentally, the outright sale of a copyright, even years after publication results in a gain and that gain is treated as taxable income. If you are an accepted non-resident the income may be non-taxable, but if you are living abroad to save tax you will anyway need more professional guidance than can be given here.

10
COPYRIGHT

10
COPYRIGHT

Your publisher generally arranges for the copyright of your book. Since a book can only be copyrighted after publication, there is no need to apply for copyright before submitting your manuscript to a publisher. Nor need you be afraid that without a copyright, the "work" will be copied or plagiarized. Trade publishers do not work that way. However, if you want to be extremely cautious in this area, merely send a copy of your manuscript by registered mail (return receipt requested) to your attorney for safekeeping.

Nevertheless there are instances in which you should be acquainted with the rules of the United States copyright law. You may want to publish your own book; or you may want to determine whether a book similar to the book you propose to do has been published and copyrighted before (copyright search); or you may want to ascertain whether there is an infringment on your rights.

A copyright is a form of protection given to an author by United States law (Title 17, U.S. Code). Under this law the author is granted the rights to print, reprint and copy the work; to sell and distribute copies of the work; and to transform and/or revise the work. Only the author or those deriving their rights through him can rightfully claim copyright. Mere ownership of a book or manuscript does not give the owner the right of copyright. In the case of works made for hire, it is the employer, and not the employee, who is regarded as the author. There is no provision for securing a blanket copyright to cover all works of an author. Each work must be copyrighted separately for complete protection.

You may copyright fiction, non-fiction, poetry, compilations, composite works, directories, catalogues, annual publications, information in tabular form, maps, works of art, reproductions of works of art, drawings, photographs and prints.

You may not copyright ideas, plans, titles, names, short phrases, slogans, account books, diaries, bank checks, score cards and the like. Nor may you copyright anything that consists entirely of information that is common property and contains no original ownership, such as, calendars, height and weight charts, schedules of sporting events, etc.

For further information on the provisions of the copyright law, write to the Register of Copyrights, Library of Congress, Washington, D.C. 20540, and request the booklet available on this subject.

Your Estate

Upon death, your copyright(s) may be willed to your beneficiary. This is accomplished by stipulating in your will your instructions, (with proper advice from your attorney). This is generally overlooked or waved aside by new authors, but it could be important.

Copyright Search

There are three ways to find out whether a work is copyrighted, and the facts of the copyright. You may merely examine the work (a cursory method at best), you may personally make a search of the Copyright Office catalogues and other records in Washington, or you may have the Copyright Office make the search for you. Most people have a busy schedule and do not have the time to go to Washington to do their own search. It is suggested that you write for Circular No. 22 from the Register of Copyrights, Washington, D.C. 20540. The complete procedure is given in that brochure. If you wish to have the Copyright Office make a search for you, they will do so on your request for a fee of $5 per hour. You must provide the Office with the following information:

1. The title of the work, with any possible variants;
2. The names of the authors, including possible pseudonyms;
3. The name of the probable copyright owner, which is frequently the publisher or producer;
4. The approximate date when the work was published or registered;
5. The type of work;
6. The registration number or any other copyright date.

They will send you an estimate of the total search fee. The Copyright Office does warn, however, that searches are not always conclusive, regardless of who makes them.

11

THE BOOK BUSINESS

THE BOOK BUSINESS

Books Are Different

One of the aims of this work has been to brush aside some of the mystique that even today is summoned around anything to do with books and "literature." Researching, writing, editing and publishing non-fiction is an everyday pursuit for many thousands of people, and as individuals one does not have a right to expect preferential consideration from the community. But the product, as distinct from ourselves, does have some claim.

Books are different from the vast range of goods in the shops in combining a physical article with ideas. The physical product is only the container for wrapping up the information and the thoughts imparted by the author; yet it often has its own aesthetic appeal. A well-designed book would, for instance, be handled with care and interest by the foreigner with no understanding of English. Very few things combine a physical article with ideas. Films do, but then the film itself cannot be handled with joy; it can only be seen through a projector. Tape recordings and records also require intermediary equipment.

152

There is also the point that books are made to last. Not only are they often beautiful in themselves, so that it hurts to see them badly handled, but the reader usually takes care of them so that they continue to be capable of giving pleasure or providing information for many years to come. Those we buy today outlast ourselves, as many of those we inherited or buy secondhand outlived their original owners. Many children are first taught to take care of books when given a pictorial or story book once used by their parents or grandparents. At the extreme, rare books are among the safest investments, though their purchase solely for the financial motive by collectors who will never appreciate their intrinsic value is a negation of their real purpose.

Authors usually do their part in promoting interest in and understanding of books—the attitude that books are different. Many—and not only publishers—are ready to attack those who say that books are "too expensive." Why are they too expensive and compared with what? What else can give such immediate and yet such lasting satisfaction as a good book, purchased for perhaps the price of a meal.

Are Authors Badly Paid?

The story that authors are among the most unfairly rewarded people in the community, that everyone from the publisher to the Secretary of the Treasury conspires to keep them down, is a well-worn thread in creative folklore. Publishers grow rich while authors toil for the' barest necessities of life; was it not once reported that the "average earnings" of an author were only $1,000 a year, and how could anyone live on that? How is it that the bookseller, who merely hands a copy of the book across the counter, makes three times as much on it as does the man who wrote it? And why should libraries be allowed to lend to dozens of readers a book on which only a single royalty is paid and which those people might otherwise have bought for themselves?

Perhaps that element of grievance is exaggerated beyond reason by people who are, after all, professional communicators.

153

One should consider:

Firstly, just who *are* "authors?" It is not unusual among non-fiction publishers to have many of their authors write in their spare time, as a supplementary activity, often on subjects arising out of their jobs and professions. Most would not wish to become full-time "professional" authors, even if they trusted their own ability to produce rapid successful books in some fields and give up other employment—though even these people often combine writing with a little part-time lecturing or other paid occupation, if only to bring themselves into contact with the wide world—but the rest usually produce better books by not doing so. Starvation level threatens only those who, with inadequate talent, knowledge or self-discipline, have turned full-time authors for the prestige of it, or to be their own master—to be, at least in theory, free from a boss, from office hours, from daily travel, or whatever it is that they feel cramps their genius. If these writers do not earn enough, by and large the remedy is in their own hands. No one is compelled to become a full-time author; the fact that you have written one or two successful books does not justify the assumption that you can do nothing but writing in the future; indeed, by renouncing another occupation you may be depriving yourself of a part of life that, for all its disadvantages, provided stimulation of a kind.

The "average earnings" of authors are sometimes too readily quoted as though they should bear comparison with those of full-time professionals such as doctors. A tendency to regard authors as a distinct class set apart in the community can lead to naivete when discussing their financial affairs.

Secondly, some authors speak of bookshops as though they are parasites, fattening on proceeds which should go elsewhere. "The bookshop gets an average of 40 per cent and I only get 10 per cent. Why?" The answer is in fact very simple. A 40% discount is common in the retail trade for articles similar to books in variety and price. Bookshops have heavy overheads including taxes, and not all the books they stock are eventually sold, while many others take a long time to find a customer. The economics of retail selling in fact mean that any lower discount would make business impossible; and as it is, many bookshops do not make enough profit to improve their premises and train fresh staff. Once you accept that the retailer needs 40%, it is obviously impossible that you as author should receive another 40% leaving the publisher with only the remaining 20% out of which to pay all production bills, his staff and other overheads and interest charges, and make a profit. A 10 per cent stake in the total price is generally not unrealistic or unfair.

Thirdly, if you read that your publisher has made a big profit, do not automatically assume it is at your expense. As in other industries, only the profitable firm succeeds, will be able to borrow money for future growth and to pay the tax bill, and will have guaranteed continuity. The author's worst fear should be of publishers that go bankrupt or sell out to larger firms who may lack any enthusiasm for the books taken over. It is bankruptcies and unsatisfactory takeovers and mergers that have really hurt many authors. Profit too, is not always what it sounds. In the present year, corporate taxes on profits are high; the profit is in fact likely to be largely assessed on the value of stock not yet sold, but the IRS of course demands cash and not books for settlement.

Fifth. Some authors say that it is not worth troubling to increase earnings since they are so heavily taxed. Unless your book sales are in the quarter-of-a-million bracket, this is not true. As was indicated in the last chapter, authors have many potential advantages from the tax point of view—if they are prepared to bother to exploit them or engage an accountant to do so. This point is emphasized here since it is so often the very people most bitter about the unprofitability of authorship who do not trouble to look after their financial matters properly. To shrug off such matters as beyond you or too much of a bore can only demonstrate to others that you are not truly competent over managing your affairs.

Publishing As a Career

Some readers of this book may be younger people who have
155

wondered about making publishing their career. For the right type of person, it can be among the most exciting of jobs, and today, is by no means as badly paid as tradition has it, though it still calls for concentrated work over longer hours than are common in most other offices.

There is no specific pre-entry training course, and a degree or other qualifications will not always gain priority, employers judging people very much for their practical ability to do the job. Basic literacy is obviously important, and flair and enthusiasm for books or for the subject matter covered may count for a lot, but just as important is the ability to grasp detail and work methodically, for publishing is a highly complex, detailed and fragmented business. Remember that very little actual research or writing is done in most publishers' offices, since most books have outside authors, and publishing is therefore not really an alternative to an academic post at a university. Otherwise the range of jobs is wide, and in most there are equal opportunities for men and women, though secretaries are normally female and representatives calling at bookshops and colleges male. In smaller firms responsibilities are often combined according to the talents available, a designer perhaps also doing estimating or production work, and an editor handling publicity; larger firms tend to work in watertight compartments. A smaller firm should therefore be more attractive to someone seeking an insight into publishing as a whole. Most small firms are quick to recognize and use talent, and switching to another job within the firm is often simple enough.

The problem, especially in small firms, is matching the supply and demand. Most publishers are inundated with inquiries from would-be employees, especially on the editorial side, but often still find it difficult to obtain the right people. Few publishers have more than one or two openings of the same kind at any time, and there are sharp differences in the requirements of different firms even for nominally-similar jobs. Females have a big advantage in making an initial entry because there is always a shortage of good secretaries or assistants. The young woman determined to make publishing her career should take a crash secretarial course even if she has a degree. Her first job might be mundane, but once inside a publisher's office she will quickly have an opportunity to prove herself. Many publishing jobs are advertised in the weekly trade magazine, *Publishers' Weekly,* though so many school and university graduates proffer their services that it is often not necessary to advertise for junior staff. He who shouts first and loudest tends to be heard most. Write in detail giving your reasons for wanting to go into publishing, to a firm of your choice, or to several firms, some months before you will be free to take a job, and offer yourself for interview. If you do not hear, send a reminder six or eight weeks later. Publishing is a branch of the communications business, and the prospective boss takes note of those who can successfully communicate their enthusiasm.

THE AUTHOR'S LIBRARY
AND
SOURCE MATERIAL

THE AUTHOR'S LIBRARY
AND
SOURCE MATERIAL

Your Own Library

The centerpiece of the author's own reference library should be an encyclopedia, ideally *Encyclopedia Britannica*, although the *Columbia Encyclopedia* (one volume) is also extremely useful. A good dictionary is of course essential, and most people's choice will be *Webster's Collegiate Dictionary*, although the larger, more expensive *Webster's International Dictionary* would undoubtedly repay the extra cost and shelf room. Also recommended are the more recent *Random House Dictionary* and *American Heritage Dictionary*, because of their completeness and modernity.

Most people writing the kind of book with which this volume deals will need a good atlas and gazetteer, if only to check exactly where a place is, how the name is spelled, or how far it lies from the next big town. The atlas volume is a substantial bonus for buyers of *Encyclopedia Britannica;* more detailed is the *Rand McNally Atlas, Webster's Geographical Dictionary,* listing over 40,000 geographical names with concise notes, solves many problems, but because of its worldwide coverage cannot

160

include most of the smallest places.

The traditional authority on points of English is H.W. Fowler's *A Dictionary of Modern American Usage*. The only book unequivocally recommended to help improve your writing ability is the classic slim volume *The Elements of Style* by William Strunk and E.B. White.

Roget's *Thesaurus* and other dictionaries of synonyms occasionally spur the mind but many authors find them not quite so useful as expected. The library should however include a good dictionary of quotations, such as a modern edition of *Bartlett's Familiar Quotations* or *The Oxford Dictionary of Quotations*.

A few other general reference works (to supplement books on his own subject) will ensure that the author can answer at least a reasonable proportion of his own queries quickly. There should be one standard history of the United States, a dictionary of dates, a classical dictionary, a technical and/or scientific dictionary, and of course an almanac, a mass of up-to-date information on innumerable topics; it is worth buying afresh each year. So is that essential reference tool especially designed for the freelance writer, *Literary Market Place*. Its range of information has increased steadily over the years. It lists not only American publishers with their likely requirements, but literary agencies, typing services, etc. The individual author cannot expect to keep up-to-date copies of all the expensive and useful annuals available (i.e. *Who's Who*) and should concentrate on those particularly relevant to his interests, turning to the local reference library for the others.

Recent years have seen the publication of a growing number of specialized dictionaries and handbooks of varying quality, and indeed the literature of many subjects, technical and other, is expanding so rapidly that it is worth making a point of borrowing or studying the newest additions in your local or institutional library, to assess their worth and to study their bibliographies. For instance, few of the numerous books published on local history during the past fifteen years are mentioned in standard encyclopedias or other reference works.

Such bibliographies of course list the traditional source books as well as newer titles, and once owning a working library of, say, an encyclopedia, twenty general and perhaps another twenty or thirty specialist books currently in print, an author will often be wise to go back to some of the earlier works long since available only secondhand. So far as money and space permit, most of us find that even second-rate reference books can come into their own, supplementing a more standard work.

Local historians and topographical writers will find books published a century or more ago especially valuable. Moreover, early travel, technical and other works have a charm of their own and may prove excellent investments if properly stored.

To keep abreast of useful literature, old and new, visits to libraries and antiquarian booksellers are obviously called for, and you can join the mailing lists of antiquarian booksellers specializing in your field. But today there is a seller's market for standard source material, and when a catalogue arrives it needs studying quickly: often orders should be sent by telegram or telephone. Remember that it is worth paying a lot more for a reference tool which has remained in demand for generations and whose price is likely to continue rising than it is for an ephemeral work of more doubtful quality. Good, scarce works will continue to appreciate—even if for argument's sake they are reprinted. Much primary source material is now being reprinted, of course, and if interested you can get your name added to the mailing lists of publishers producing substantial lists.

Use of Other Libraries

Public libraries perform two main functions. They lend a wide range of books for the reader to use at home; and they keep another range to be consulted in their own buildings. Many authors make surprisingly little use of both services and indeed fail to understand just what facilities are at their command.

162

The local branch of your public library has a lending department, from which any card holder can select books either for study or for light reading. But that is only the tip of the iceberg. The librarian will also be pleased to obtain any work you need for study purposes that is available for loan at a library anywhere in the library system.

Some expensive reference works and most very rare books of course do not leave library premises. An expensive annual stocked by the larger libraries which has special value to authors is *Subject Guide To Books In Print*. It contains both author and title indexes, so that you can check whether any other books are available with titles similar to the one you have dreamed up—indeed that your proposed title has not already been used—and can see if a book published years ago is still in print. *British Books in Print* should also be found in the larger libraries. Big libraries will also have *The Dictionary of Biography*, as well as the current *Who's Who*, and back issues of standard reference works. There may be old newspaper files (sometimes also available for consultation at the office of the newspaper or its successor), runs of magazines old or new, maps and collections of photographs. The best libraries may have some kind of index to their collections of printed and photographic material of local interest. Most city and state offices now have established record files and many have built up substantial collections of documents and records.

To some extent your local library should also be able to act as signpost to the greater resources of the national institutions, such as the National Academy of Sciences, National Institutes of Health, Smithsonian Institution, National Aeronautics and Space Administration and Academy of Medicine, which not only have substantial collections of their own but will often give guidance to the *bona fide* author. It is usually better to write in advance, stating what you want and why, rather than to call without warning and have your inquiry handled by whomever happens to be on duty. It is always worth emphasizing that you are writing a book and mentioning the publisher if that has been fixed; most libraries and institutions are worried by a stream of less serious inquirers wanting information to settle bets or to produce school essays. Even the busiest administrators have time to spare to guide the author who seeks specific guidance, as opposed to students who write asking for "all you know" on a wide subject.

The Library of Congress, for serious inquirers, is prepared to complete the formalities and with a fair amount of time at their disposal.

Keeping Abreast of Your Subject

The successful author must keep abreast of the changes, which above all means knowing just what other books and papers on his subject have been published. The obvious course is to subscribe to the specialist magazines, to run through the back numbers and to join any appropriate organizations in order to receive their journals or other publications even if not actively to take part in meetings and courses. Note what secondhand booksellers, publishers and other suppliers advertise in the magazines and journals. You may be lucky enough to have a bookseller who will keep you informed of new titles appearing on your subject; indeed some authors deliberately obtain their new books by mail from one of the top dozen or so academic booksellers in order to receive catalogues listing new titles and brochures of new series.

The *New York Times Book Review* can be a useful investment for the author wanting to keep abreast of the publishing and literary scene as a whole. Only a few books of the kind dealt with here receive long reviews in the body of the paper, but many more are given short notices and most titles are advertised by their publishers. For those more interested in the trade, *Publishers' Weekly* lists all new books published each week and again contains many publishers' advertisements. The special spring and fall issues list most of the books to be published during the following six months. Few magazines now give

164

a complete review coverage of all books published in their fields, and while the learned journals tend to review a greater range of titles, their notices often appear too late to be useful. The popular press review only a small selection of books in total and only a small proportion of these are definitive non-fiction.

Many authors lose interest in a subject after publishing a book on it. The trouble comes when the first edition sells out and the publisher asks if there are any revisions for a reprint. Even if your main interest changes, if you would like your book to be reprinted (however unlikely that might appear when you receive your first royalty statement) do something to keep abreast of changes, if only by noting down the titles of books and papers that must be consulted.

Storing Your Material

The best books are often those based on material collected over a long period—material gleaned from other books, from original records, newspaper cuttings, magazine files, interviews with old people, and often from many other sources as well. It is all too easy for the part-time author to be so swamped by paper by the time he comes to start writing that he wastes valuable energy looking for what should be handy—or finds he has no identification details of a paper he once read and must consult. Introduce a simple filing and recording system. Everyone has his own method, and the best are not elaborate, but do something to prevent waste and muddle. A simple card index listing where main references to topics may be found (in books, newspaper cuttings, transcriptions of notes and the like) can be useful. A cunningly simple device is a photocopy of the index of the principal existing work on the subject with wide margins in which you can indicate the whereabouts of the notes and other material you hold. Newspaper clippings are a particular curse if not stuck in a scrap book or properly filed—and the paragraph in today's paper which you stow away carefully could solve an otherwise elusive problem when you come to write in eighteen months' time. The most recent developments and problems can sometimes prove the hardest to unravel, simply because they have not had time to be documented.

SPECIMEN CONTRACT

SPECIMEN CONTRACT

Publishing contracts vary somewhat, but some general
policies apply to all. Rather than offer a hybrid made up of many
contracts, here is an actual contract from a reputable New York
publishing house. The notes and comments listed after the
specimen contract consist of advice to the author before signing.
Should you be offered a contract which contains clauses that are
far removed in intent from the contract shown below, consult an
attorney before signing. Also keep in mind that the amounts and
percentages in this speciment contract are merely illustrations.
Each publisher will naturally decide his own in relation to his
own circumstances and general practice.

If it is desired to add riders to individual clauses or change
the wording of a standard contract, each change or rider should
be initialed by both author and publisher.

AGREEMENT made this . . . . day of . . . . , 19 . . . .
between . . . . of . . . . ,

hereinafter called the "Publisher" and . . . .
hereinafter called the "Author."

2. 1. The Author hereby grants and assigns to the Publisher the exclusive right to
publish, print, reprint, take out copyright, renew copyright and vend a certain work now
tentatively entitled . . . .
(hereinafter referred to as the "Work"), in any and all languages throughout the world,
together with all subsidiary and additional rights pertaining thereto. Such rights shall
enure to the Publisher during the term or terms of copyright and any renewals thereof.

2. Copyright shall be taken out in the United States in the name of the Publisher, at
the sole expense of the Publisher.

3. The Publisher shall pay to or upon the order of the Author royalties based on the
retail price received by publisher, on all copies of the regular trade edition sold by the
Publisher and paid for, less returns, as follows:

> 10% on the first 5,000 copies sold
> 12-1/2% on the next 5,000 copies sold
> 15% on all copies sold over 10,000

except that:

a) on any sales at discounts of fifty per cent (50%) of the list price, or more, the
Publisher shall pay the Author the stipulated royalty which shall be calculated on the net
amount received by the Publisher;

b) on shipments made to points outside the continental United States the
Publisher shall pay one-half (1/2) of the stipulated royalties thereby providing for any
extra shipping, duty, postage and handling costs;

c) where the Publisher has made advertising allowance to a dealer for special
promotion or sale of the Work, or on sales made as a result of special mail order advertising, the Publisher shall pay one-half (1/2) of the stipulated royalties;

d) on all sales of sheets, the percentage of royalty shall be the same as for bound
books and shall be calculated on the net amount received by the Publisher; and

e) no royalties shall be paid on copies sold to or furnished gratis to the Author, or
furnished for review, bonus, advertising, sample or like purpose; or on copies that are
defective, unsalable, or destroyed.

4. (a) The subsidiary and additional rights referred to in paragraph 1 hereof include
the rights set forth below, and the net proceeds of sale thereof, if any, after deducting all
direct expenses incurred by the Publisher in connection therewith, shall be shared by the
Author and Publisher in the percentages indicated:

	To Author	To Publisher
1) Abridgement, condensation, excerpts, extras and anthology	50%	50%
2) First periodical (publication in periodical form before book publication)	50%	50%
3) Second periodical (publication in pamphlets, compilations, magazines, newspapers or other books after book publication)	50%	50%
4) Publication rights to Book Clubs or similar organizations and paperback editions (whether for a lump sum or otherwise)	50%	50%

5) The right to sell, lease or license
   for use throughout the world:
   (a) Dramatic rights 50%   50%
   (b) Motion picture rights 50%   50%
   (c) Radio and television rights 50%   50%
   (d) Mechanical reproduction rights 50%   50%
   (e) Microfilming 50%   50%
   (f) Brailling 50%   50%
   (g) Commercial rights 50%   50%

6) Sale of rights to publish, in whole or
   part, in countries outside the United
   States (including translation rights) 50%   50%

7) All rights not otherwise specified
   in this agreement, whether or not
   now in existence 50%   50%

(b) All such rights may be granted by the Publisher, whether by sale, license, or otherwise, and the Publisher for that purpose is constituted the attorney-in-fact of the Author. The Author agrees to sign, make, execute, deliver, and acknowledge all such papers, documents, and agreements as may be necessary to effectuate the grants hereinabove contemplated, and to do all things necessary thereto. In the event that the Author shall fail to sign, make, execute, deliver, and acknowledge such papers, they may be signed, executed, delivered and acknowledged by the Publisher as the attorney-in-fact of the Author with the same force and effect as if signed by the Author. All agreements made by the Publisher for the disposition of such rights shall be available for reasonable inspection of the Author.

5. The Author represents and warrants (a) that the Work as submitted is original; (b) that he is the sole author and proprietor thereof and has full power to enter into this agreement; (c) that the Work has not heretofore been published, in whole or in part, in book form or otherwise; (d) that he has not entered into or become subject to any contract, agreement or understanding with respect thereto other than this agreement; and (e) that the Work is innocent and contains no matter which, if published, will be libelous, lewd, obscene or scandalous, in violation of any right of privacy, or otherwise injurious, or which will infringe upon any proprietary right at common law or any statutory copyright or any Penal Law. The Author agrees to indemnify and hold the Publisher harmless against any suit, claim, demand or recovery by reason of any violation of any of the foregoing representations and warranties or by reason of any violation of proprietary right or copyright, any invasion of right of privacy or other right, or any injurious or libelous matter in the Work, actual or claimed, including, but not by way of limitation, all expenses, amounts paid in settlement before or after suit is begun, court costs and attorneys' fees. If in the Publisher's opinion the Work shall contain any matter which, if published, would be libelous or otherwise injurious or would violate any right of privacy or other right, or would infringe on any right at common law or any statutory copyright, the Publisher shall be under no obligation to publish the Work and the Author shall forthwith return to the Publisher any amounts which the Publisher may have advanced to him. Publication of the Work however shall not be deemed a waiver of the foregoing indemnities.

6. The Author shall not, while the Work is in print, without the written consent of the Publisher, write, print or publish, or cause to be written, printed or published, any revised, corrected, enlarged or abridged version of the Work, or in any way assist or be interested in any such version or in any book or publication of a character that might interfere with or reduce the sales of the Work.

7. The Author will, upon the Publisher's request, do all acts necessary to protect the

copyright, renewals thereof and all rights pertaining to the Work. The Publisher shall have the right to bring any action or proceeding in the name of the Publisher or in the name of the Author for the enjoining of any infringement of the copyright or other rights and for any damages resulting therefrom. The net amount recovered in any such action or proceeding, or in settlement thereof, after deducting all expenses incident thereto, shall be divided between the Author and the Publisher in accordance with the percentages hereinabove in this agreement set forth, in the same manner as though permission had been given by the Publisher for the infringing work.

8. The author shall deliver to the Publisher, not later than the ...... day of ...., 19......; a complete, legible, final copy of the manuscript acceptable and satisfactory to the Publisher in content and form, including all drawings, charts and designs which in the opinion of the Publisher are necessary parts of the Work. The Author shall also deliver to the Publisher an index, if required, promptly after proof is available for making the index. If the Author fails to supply all such drawings, charts, designs and index, the Publisher may have them made and charge the expense thereof against the Author. The provision of this paragraph as to the character, condition and time of receipt of such copy are of the essence of this agreement, and in the event of the Author's default hereunder, the Publisher may, at its option, decline to publish the Work, whereupon the Author shall forthwith return to the Publisher any amounts which it may have advanced to him. In such event, if the manuscript should be completed subsequently, the Author shall nevertheless be obligated to offer the same to the Publisher, which, at its option, shall have the right to publish the same upon the terms of this agreement.

Any expense incurred by the Publisher in excess of $25 in making any alterations or corrections in any proofs from final copy shall, if made pursuant to the Author's direction, be borne by the Author and charged against the Author.

9. Should the Author incorporate in the Work any writings or other matter previously published, either of his or of any other writer or artist, he shall obtain and deliver to the Publisher proper and complete written permission and authorization to reprint the same from the owner of the copyright thereof.

10. All matters concerning editing and revising of the text and illustrations, the manner of publication, production, design, distribution, advertising and publicity, shall be left to the discretion of the Publisher, which shall bear all the expense of publication, distribution, manufacture and advertising. The Publisher shall publish the Work in such style, at such price and under such title as it may deem advisable.

11. If the Publisher at any time has unsold or returned copies of the Work on hand which, in the Publisher's judgment, could not be sold at regular trade discounts and on usual terms within a reasonable time, or if the Publisher, in the exercise of reasonable discretion, determines that existing conditions warrant it, the Publisher may sell copies of the Work at the best price obtainable, and if such price is below cost, no royalties shall be payable to the Author on such sales.

12. Subsequent to the publication of the Work, the Publisher may publish a cheap edition thereof under any of its own imprints and, if the retail price thereof shall be less than fifty per cent (50%) of the retail price of the latest printing, shall pay the Author a royalty of five per cent (5%) of the cheap edition retail price, subject to the exceptions set forth in paragraph 3 above.

13. The Publisher may lease the plates or negatives of the Work or sell reprint rights to another publisher or to a book club or similar organization, and shall in that event pay the Author fifty per cent (50%) of the net amount received therefor, after deduction of the cost of plates, if any, and/or other direct expenses.

14. The Publisher shall furnish the Author six copies of the Work as published free of charge. Any and all additional copies requested by the Author shall be furnished to him at a discount of 40% from the retail price. The Author may, if he desires, resell sucho

copies to individuals at the full retail price, but may not sell to libraries, schools, bookstores, retail stores, book dealers or organizations. If the Author makes any sales in violation of this provision, the Publisher shall not be required to furnish the Author with any further copies and may use any remedies provided by law.

15. The Publisher shall render to the Author, or his duly authorized representatives, in April and October of each year, statements of book sales made and royalties earned and of rights granted and fees received during the six-months' period ending the preceding December 31st and June 30th respectively, and shall accompany such statements with checks in settlement, provided, however, that the Publisher shall have the right to set off against such sums any returns to the date of such statements. Whenever sales in any six month period fall below one-hundred (100) copies, no accounting need be rendered until the semi-annual settlement date following the sale of a total of one-hundred (100) copies.

16. All payments made by the Publisher to the Author, whether under this agreement or not, shall be chargeable against and recoverable from any or all monies accruing to the Author under this agreement and/or all other agreements between the parties or their assigns. Where the Author has received an overpayment of royalties or other sums, or is otherwise indebted to the Publisher, the Publisher may deduct the amount thereof from any further royalties or other sums, whether payable on this or other books by the Author which may be published by the Publisher, it being understood, however, that the term "overpayment" does not apply to an unearned advance specifically agreed to as applying to one work.

17. Whenever, at any time after two years from the date of publication, demand for the Work, in the opinion of the Publisher, shall be insufficient to render its continued publication profitable, and the Publisher shall so notify the Author by mail to his last address on the Publisher's records, the Author shall have the option to purchase from the Publisher all of the rights granted hereunder at a reasonable price to be agreed upon. If the Author fails to exercise such option within thirty (30) days after the giving of such notice, (a) the Publisher may thereafter dispose of such rights, in whole or in part, as it sees fit, and in such case shall pay the Author one-half of the amounts which would otherwise be payable to him for the sale of such rights in accordance with this agreement, and (b) the Publisher shall be free of any further obligation hereunder except for the payment of royalties which have accrued to the date of such notice.

The Author shall also have the option, exercisable within sixty (60) days after the Publisher gives the aforesaid notice, to purchase as an entirety, all bound copies of the Work on hand at twenty-five per cent (25%) of the catalogue retail price, all sheet copies at twelve per cent (12%) of the catalogue retail price, and the plates (if plates were made and if they have not already been melted) at twenty-five per cent (25%) of their original cost. Should the Author fail to exercise this option, the Publisher may dispose of the properties as it sees fit, without obligation to make any payments to the Author in connection therewith.

18. If the Publisher allows the Work to go out of print and the Author notifies the Publisher in writing to reprint the Work, the Author shall have the rights provided for in paragraph 17 hereof, such rights to be exercised within 30 and 60 days respectively, after such notice, unless the Publisher agrees to reprint the work within six months thereafter.

19. The Author grants the Publisher the option to publish the Author's next two works of 10,000 words or more or the Author's next two art or juvenile books, as the case may be, upon the same terms and conditions as are set forth in this agreement, such option to be exercised within thirty (30) days after the submission to the Publisher of the complete manuscripts of such works.

20. The performance by the Publisher of the terms and conditions of this agreement on its part to be performed is subject to shortages of governmental restrictions on essential materials and supplies, delays by the Author, acts of war, strikes or other

conditions beyond the control of the Publisher.

21. Regardless of the place of execution and delivery of this agreement, it shall be interpreted and construed in accordance with and governed by the laws of the State of New York.

22. This agreement contains the whole understanding of the parties, supersedes all previous oral or written representations or agreements with respect to the Work and may not be changed, modified or discharged orally.

23. The terms of this agreement shall apply to all works of the Author submitted to and accepted for publication by the Publisher as though the titles thereof were hereinabove in paragraph 1 set forth, subject to any modification which may be agreed upon by the parties in writing with respect to a particular work.

24. The Publisher may have the manuscript of the Work rewritten or added to or illustrated by anyone designated by the Publisher and approved by the Author and such person shall be known as co-author of the Work. Any payments provided for in paragraphs 3,4,12, and 13 hereof to be made to the Author shall be divided by the Publisher between the Author and co-author in the properties of ....% to the Author and ....% to the co-author.

25. The Publisher may have the Work illustrated by anyone designated by the Publisher and approval by the author, and shall charge the Author therefor a sum not exceeding $........

26. Record is made of the fact that the undersigned Author is actually co-author of the Work with .... and that .... shall be entitled to receive from the Publisher ....% of any payments to be made to the Author, under paragraphs 3, 4, 12, and 13 hereof.

27. The Author may assign his rights but not his obligations under this agreement upon written notice to the Publisher. The Publisher may assign any right granted to the Publisher hereunder but may not, without the written consent of the Author (which shall not be unreasonably withheld) assign this agreement as an entirety except in connection with the sale or transfer of its whole business or any department thereof.

28. This agreement shall be binding upon and enure to the benefit of the parties and their heirs, executors, administrators, successors and, except as herein provided, their assigns.

29. An advance against future royalties of $............ shall be paid as follows:

   $............ on execution of this contract
   $............ on acceptance of the completed manuscript
     or
   $............ on publication

  IN WITNESS WHEREOF, the parties have executed this agreement the day and year first above written.

....
Author

....
Publisher

....
Witness

....
Witness

....
Date

....
Date

174

Specimen Contract, Notes and Comments

Clause 2. This entitles the publisher to register a copyright in his name. In most instances if the author insists on having the copyright in his name, the publisher will agree.

Clause 3. There are instances when royalties are paid on the net price (actual cash received by publisher) rather than the retail price of the book. This usually occurs with text and technical books.

As stated in the chapter on royalties, paperbacks and some other types of books very often bear a royalty less than 10%.

Clause 4a; If subsidiary rights have been sold through a literary agent the cost of the fees involved are usually shared by the author and publisher. (The same applies to any legal costs which were incurred in the course of negotiating a contract.)

Clause 4a5. Fiction writers please note that the common practice regarding movie rights is fast becoming 75% to the author and 25% to the publisher.

Clause 8. The delivery date of the manuscript is usually agreed to prior to signing. Authors should be very realistic about this commitment since this clause contains a default provision which the publisher can invoke. In the case of an unfinished manuscript, the advance must be returned by the author in all of the listed instances of *default*, but *not* if the manuscript does not meet the editorial standards (intangible) of the publisher after the fact. The insertion of this clause gives the publisher an "out" which he should not have after the author has completed the work.

Note in this clause the penalty for author's alterations payable by the publisher. Any costs in excess of this amount (amount may vary) are deductible from the author's royalties.

Clause 14. Six free copies of an average priced hardbound book is normal. Paperback publishers sometimes offer twelve. In the case of an expensive art or specialized book the contract may call for four copies.

There are some special cases where the author may be permitted to buy copies for resale. These may entail authors who

175

are special teachers or lecturers using the book for this purpose and authors who are specialists in a particular field and have a subsidiary business in this field, etc.

The author should discuss this with the publisher prior to signing to make certain that a 40% discount will be granted for special purposes which may exist.

Clause 15.   These dates for submission of royalty reports may vary, but in most cases reports should be sent semi-annually.

A new practice is fast developing in the publishing industry which allows the publisher to withhold a percentage of royalties against future returns.

Clause 19.   The clause giving the publisher first right of refusal of the author's subsequent work or works is gradually going out of style. It is not in the best interests of the author. Publishers who really want your current work will generally not object too strenuously to the deletion of this clause.

Clause 20.   This matter was discussed earlier in the book. However, "conditions beyond the control of the publisher" is a loosely worded provision, and on occasion has been used as a loophole by the publisher for whatever reason, to avoid producing the work. Some publishers will commit themselves to a firm publication date (usually within 24 months of receipt of the accepted manuscript). The author should attempt to get a contractual commitment, if possible. If this commitment is obtained and the publisher does not meet his deadline, the author has the right to request return of the manuscript without having to return the advance.

14

AUTHOR'S ALTERATIONS

14

AUTHOR'S ALTERATIONS

Author's alterations are costly and cause delays. It is always very tempting to make alterations in the proof stage. You can delete a word here, change a phrase there, and put in a comma somewhere else. It seems so simple. But in truth, each alteration or addition means laborious work for the typesetter and expensive for the author and the publisher. If typesetting costs are increased substantially, the publisher's chance of making the book pay is reduced because he must either raise the price of the book or sell a larger number of copies to cover costs.

It takes great care and skill to set type properly. But much of it must be undone again on each page in order to accommodate the smallest alteration. It is to everyone's advantage that you make all changes while the work is still in manuscript form and not after it is typeset.

Every alteration made in a proof means higher typesetting costs (if the rate of corrections exceeds a certain percentage these costs will be charged to the account of the author). No less important they mean a delay which may result in the postponement of publication date.

Author's alterations should be kept to the absolute minimum: galleys and page proofs are intended for checking, not for alteration. It has been said that authors would dispense with most of their alterations if they had to pay on the spot for making them. There is more than a grain of truth to this.

Too often an author thinks "Oh, never mind, I can always alter it on the proof." This attitude is disastrous—it leads immediately to extra costs.

A few words, or even letters, added or deleted may mean the respacing of a large number of words by the typesetter. Or it could entail the resetting of the entire paragraph. You can help to keep costs down by following these three rules:

1. Type your script using one side of the paper in double spacing. Number the pages.

2. Check your typescript. Make sure you have written what you mean, that you have eliminated any inconsistency in style, and that your punctuation, capitalization and spelling are correct.

3. Learn the art of proof reading. Always use the standard marks of proof correction as shown in the chart below. These symbols are clear, unambiguous, and understood by all typesetters. Their use will become second nature to you in a very short time.

PROOFREADER'S MARKS

℘	Delete
℘̂	Delete and close up
℘	Reverse
⌒	Close up
#	Insert space
⌒/#	Close up and insert space
¶	Paragraph
□	Indent 1 em
⊏	Move to left
⊐	Move to right
⊔	Lower
⊓	Raise
∧	Insert marginal addition
V∧	Space evenly
✗	Broken letter—used in margin
↓	Push down space
=	Straighten line
‖	Align type
∧	Insert comma
V̇	Insert apostrophe
V̈	Insert quotation mark
=/	Insert hyphen

em/	Insert em dash
en/	Insert en dash
⌃	Insert semicolon
⊙	Insert colon and en quad
⊙	Insert period and en quad
?/	Insert interrogation point
?	Query to author—in margin
⌒	Use ligature
SP	Spell out
tr	Transpose
wf	Wrong font
bf	Set in **boldface** type
rom	Set in (roman) type
ital	Set in *italic* type
caps	Set in CAPITALS
sc	Set in SMALL CAPITALS
lc	Set in lower case
✗	Lower-case letter
stet	Let it stand; restore words crossed out
no ¶	Run in same paragraph
ld in⟩	Insert lead between lines
hr #	Hair space between letters

Where an alteration *is essential*, try to make it in such a way that a minimum amount of extra work is involved. For instance, where it is necessary to add a word, try to delete a word or words of about the same number of letters: if it is necessary to delete a word try to add a word. Similarly, if you add a line, try to knock out a line, even if it is a line of only one word, otherwise the whole paragraph may have to be reset. That is part of the art of copy-editing.

All corrections should be distinct and made in ink in the margins; marks made in the text should be those indicating the place to which the correction refers.

Where several corrections occur in one line, they should be divided between the left and right margins, the order being from left to right in both margins and the individual marks should be separated by a concluding mark.

When an alteration is desired in a character, word, or words, the existing character, word, or words should be struck through and the character to be substituted written in the margin, followed by a concluding stroke (/).

Where it is desired to change one character only to a capital letter, the word "cap" should be written in the margin. Where, however, it is desired to change more than one character, or a word or words, in a particular line, to capitals, then one marginal reference "caps" should suffice, with the appropriate symbols made in the text as required.

Normally, only matter actually to be inserted or added to the existing text should be written on the proof. If, however, any comments or instructions are written on the proof, they should be encircled and preceded by the word *TYPESETTER* (in capital and underlined).

INDEX

INDEX